# Devlin

# Devlin

## Angela K Parker

*Devlin*
Copyright © 2022 by Angela K. Parker
All Rights Reserved.

Published: Angela K. Parker 2022
angelaparkerauthor@gmail.com

"Cover Design ©Angela K Parker"
**ISBN:** 9798355716844

~

For anyone feeling passed over, know that you are enough.

# Contents

# Chapter 1

**Evelyn**

"IF YOU STARE harder, I'll start to sink in."

My eyes snap to Devlin's, and he stares at me expectantly, waiting for a response.

Devlin Hughes is one of the Brand Managers at M&S Toys with me. He's smart and handsome. But he's also the biggest pain in my life.

When Devlin and I first met, I wanted him for myself, but it didn't take long to figure out that my thinking was all wrong on so many levels. One day to be exact. From the moment he opened his mouth, I knew there was something about him that would spark a fire in me. And as he spoke that

1

first day, my friendly fire turned to rage. All thoughts of us flew out the window. He would've been perfect had he not said anything, and my fantasy would still be alive.

"If your ego gets any bigger, it will burst," I fire back.

I am not in the mood for Devlin today. He never uses the breakroom at work. I'm convinced someone put him on this earth to annoy me. The only reason I came in here was for a little peace.

My relationship of five years has been on thin ice for the past year, and the argument I had with John this morning was the pick that finally broke it. He packed his things and left me with a mix of emotions. I didn't know whether to be relieved or upset. Since I came to work, I've settled on a healthy serving of pissed, and Devlin landed on the wrong side of my plate.

"My ego is just fine," Devlin says with a slick smirk and a wink. He turns his body to face me, leaning against the tall table across from me and crossing his legs at the ankles.

I glance down below his waist and back up without thinking, and he chuckles. I'm in a *report to HR* mood today, but it wouldn't be fair after what I just did.

*My stupid, stupid eyes.*

*His stupid, stupid good looks.*

"Your ego…. Your ego…." *Ugh!* "You know what, Devlin? I can't do this with you today." I can't even come up with a witty comeback after glancing at his ego, which is substantial, might I add. He'd be just the cure for my month-long dry spell if I didn't loathe his womanizing ways as I do. It's a wonder our work relationship is on point, but as soon as work is off the table, all bets are off.

Devlin eyes me curiously. Then he walks over to my table and sits across from me. "I can see that you're in a mood."

I roll my eyes at him. "I'm not in a mood," I snapped.

"You're in a mood," Devlin says. "And I have just the cure."

*Are you reading my mind?*

I lean forward a fraction, balling the hand on my lap while my other hand pauses on the handle of my coffee mug. "Whatever cure you think you have, Devlin, it's not for me." I'm not blind to the variety of women he's had over the years, and I refuse to be one of them. "Look, I just got out of a relationship. The last thing I need is another problem."

"You have me all wrong, Eve. The last thing I want is to swap spit and do unspeakable things with you." Devlin smiles, wiggling his brows. Even when he's trying to be serious, he's not. "You look like you could use a pick me up. I'm merely suggesting that we go out for drinks after work. You can even invite the ex if you should miraculously patch things up before tonight. We could even discuss the project if you're worried about content."

I want to ask him what he means by unspeakable things,

but I'm slightly annoyed that he doesn't want to sleep with me. My mind is all types of screwed up, and I want to blame it on John, but I'm not sure he's the problem in this instance.

"That is not a good idea."

"Are you afraid that you won't be able to hold your composure?" Devlin lifts an eyebrow, and I do the same. "I get it. I'm a lot to take in, but you've held your own well while working together. Surely, you're not bothered by being alone with me."

*Challenge accepted.*

He's right. I need a pick-me-up, and I would be secretly enjoying this cat and mouse game we're playing if it weren't for my ex.

"I'm in." I lift my mug to my mouth, taking a long sip while peering at him over the top and wondering what I'm getting myself into. Devlin is trouble with a capital T, and I'm asking for it.

I'VE NEVER HAD a workday that flew by so fast. Before I realized the time, it was eight after five, and I glanced up at my doorway to the sound of Devlin's smooth voice.

"Any word from the ex yet?" Devlin asked, his full frame practically covering the entrance to my office.

"Huh?" I responded, confused by his sudden appearance.

"The ex. Is he tagging along?" Devlin raised a brow.

4

I had forgotten about Devlin's offer to invite John, mainly because there was no chance of us getting back together.

"No. It's just us." I clear my throat at the intimacy of the word *us*. "It's just you and me."

Devlin chuckles. "In that case, I'll pick you up from your place in an hour." He turns to leave.

"Wait," I call after him, and he turns back toward me. "How do you know where I live?"

Devlin shrugs. "I followed you home one night," he answered. Then he's gone, leaving me with my mouth hanging open.

"Creep," I muttered.

*Creep that I just agreed to have drinks with.*

For some reason, that excites me.

Does that make me a creep too?

I shook the thought and finished the task I was working on. Then I gathered my belongings and left.

The closer I got to home as I drove, my anticipation spiked with each turn of the tires.

John is the only man I've been with outside of work for half a decade, and I chose Devlin to pop that cherry.

My home feels a little less crowded when I step inside. There's not one physical trace of John in sight. Although the memories are still fresh in my mind in every room, I ignore them.

I've spent most of my time since John left wondering where we went wrong, and this house doesn't help matters when I'm trying to forget. It will get easier as time passes, but tonight is not that night.

I want to wash my brain out for even thinking about it, but I'm glad Devlin invited me out. Maybe he will surprise me and won't be as bad as I think he is.

My best friend, Holland, would flip if he knew I agreed to go out with Devlin, even if it was innocent.

I take my black four-inch heels off, thinking about changing out of the silver and black dress I'm wearing. Then I put them back on deciding against it. The last thing I need is Devlin thinking I made an effort for him.

I walk slowly to the front door when the bell rings and open it after peering outside.

Devlin is still in his work attire—gray suit pants and a white buttoned-up long-sleeved shirt with a gray tie. The only thing missing is his gray jacket. I guess we had the same idea. Something about that makes me smile. It makes this feel less like a date.

"You're early," I noticed, focusing on Devlin's eyes because looking elsewhere is out of the question. I made that mistake earlier, and the last thing I need to think about is the log between his legs.

"The early bird always gets the worm," Devlin says with a wink. His eyes rise to look over my shoulder, making me feel exposed. I feel like he can see everything that happened inside my home, everything I don't want the world to know.

"I'm ready if you are," I said, drawing his eyes to mine.

"Eager. I like that," Devlin says smugly.

"What's that supposed to mean?"

Devlin shrugs. "It's an enticing quality, just how I like my women."

"Let's get one thing straight before we go," I quipped, crossing my arms over my chest. "This does not make me one of your women. Got it?"

"Got it," Devlin grins. "Besides, you're not my type."

I hate it when he says things like that. It makes me want to test his theory just to prove him wrong.

"I'll meet you in the car," I said, pretending to be unphased by his comment.

Devlin chuckles as he walks away toward his Benz while I grab my purse and lock up.

A couple of minutes later, I settle onto the passenger seat of Devlin's car, aware that he's watching my every move.

I look at Devlin to ask what he's staring at, but the words are trapped in my throat. I got caught up in his gaze, entranced in his darkness. I've looked into his deep brown eyes before, but he never looked at me the way he did at that moment before.

Devlin's expression changes quickly, and I wonder if I imagined it.

"Buckle up, Eve. It's going to be a wild ride," Devlin says, keeping his eyes on me for a few seconds longer before turning away.

I look away from him, too, thinking I need to get a grip.

"Where are we going anyway?" I ask, pulling the seatbelt across my shoulder and buckling it.

Devlin glances at me as he pulls away, and I realize I should've asked the question before getting into his car.

"Have you ever not been in control, Eve?"

I turn my head toward Devlin, and a smile curves his lips. "Have you?"

I'm too cowardly to ask what he means. So, I face forward again. A long quiet pause stretches between us until I can't stand it any longer.

"Do you mind?" I ask, gesturing to the radio.

"Be my guest." Devlin stops at a light while I flip through stations.

A few seconds later, a horn blows behind us, alarming me. When I look up, there are more than a few feet between us and the car ahead.

Devlin pulls off, and I ask, "Did you fall asleep at the wheel? Maybe you should let me drive."

Devlin gives me a half-smile, glancing my way and back on the road. "There you go again with your control issues."

"I don't have issues," I said through gritted teeth.

I settle on a station when I stumble upon one of my

favorites. Usually, I'd sing along, but not today—not while Devlin is in earshot.

I turn the music up—a clear sign that I don't want to engage in the conversation now—and gaze out the passenger window. We travel through two more stoplights before Devlin turns down a city street.

I rest my head on the seat and close my eyes, thinking about John and how screwed up we had become. I should've ended things months ago when he started to pull away. I loved John, but I wasn't in love with him. The only reason I didn't end our relationship was that I loved my comfort zone. It was simpler to stay in it than to start over. and look at me now. I'm starting over.

I remain quiet and keep my eyes closed for the rest of the drive.

"We're here," Devlin announced minutes later.

My eyes ease open as I stretch my arms in front of me. "Where exactly is here?" I ask, staring as Devlin drives into an open garage. I look back, attempting to glimpse my surroundings, but all I can see is a crisp white cement driveway outlined with grass that looks too green to be real. I inhale a breath as the garage door traps us inside under the cover of darkness. I look at Devlin for an explanation, and his eyes seem to glisten as he stares back at me.

"Where are we, Devlin? I thought we were going out for drinks," I said, slightly annoyed and panicked.

Sure, I see Devlin for hours on end practically every day. And sure, we've worked on many projects together, but I don't *know him,* know him. For all I know, he could be a murderer, and I didn't tell anyone where I was going or who I would be with.

"Do you trust me?" Devlin asks, and my eyes widen.

"Hell no, I don't trust you. Maybe if you had taken me to a bar like a normal person instead of bringing me here." My arms flail toward the windshield.

"Eve," Devlin says smoothly, catching my wrist in midair. "Relax. Let me take the reins. If only just once, ditch your comfort zone and venture with me."

I love his words. Why do I love his words? Why do I appreciate the silk of his voice?

"Come on," Devlin continues, releasing my wrist. "I promise there are drinks inside better than any place I could've taken you. Trust me. You *will* be satisfied." He opens his door and steps out of the car, closing it behind him. He walks over to the house door, using his key to open it, and steps inside, leaving me in the dark with my mouth hung open again.

# Chapter 2

**Devlin**

I'VE BEEN WAITING a long time to get Evelyn Parrish alone. She's the most infuriating woman I've ever met, and I've been lying to myself from the first time our eyes locked. She was not my type, but I would make an exception for her.

Eve began working at MS Toys a few months after I came on board. By that time, I had established a repertoire with the staff. Most women ogled me like a shiny toy, but I never gave them the time of day, mainly because of the whole fraternization clause. I couldn't be their boss and *be their boss.* But Eve was different. She and I were on an equal playing field. The rules didn't apply. At least, not yet.

Eve was smart as a whip, top of her class, and came highly recommended. She was the perfect complement to what I brought to the table, so I chose her to be on my team. Of course, she doesn't know that. Otherwise, she may have bolted the moment she found out. Our first meeting wasn't exactly great. I told her she was wound tight and she needed to let loose. From that point on, she's done the opposite of my suggestion.

Eve was my equal in all things professional, but from that moment, I knew she would never allow anything to blossom between us. Besides, I wouldn't attempt it anyway because she miraculously started dating someone else two weeks later.

I like to think that Eve couldn't handle the tension between us. So, she put an obstacle in our way. And now, according to her, that obstacle is gone. For years, I've waited for her to drop that low life, John. She wasn't happy. It was obvious in the way she would mention his name.

I could've stepped in long ago, but I'm not a homewrecker. Eve's decision has to be hers and hers alone when it comes to me.

I step inside my home, leaving the door to the garage wide open. I smile, thinking about the look on Eve's face when I left her in the car. I drop my keys on the bar in the kitchen, turning my back, propping my elbows on top, and leaning against it. My eyes focus on the door as I wait for Eve to emerge. She must think I'm crazy for bringing her here, but I'm anything but. I saw a chance, and I'm taking it.

The car door clicks closed a few seconds later. Then, Eve crossed the threshold shortly after. She closes the door, steps further inside, and explores her surroundings. When her eyes land on me, she stops.

"Do you live here?" Eve asks.

"I thought it was obvious, but yes. I do." I remain where I am, letting my eyes roam over her from head to toe, and back up to meet her eyes.

Eve clears her throat, flattening a palm on her belly. "I didn't picture you as the *homey* type," she says.

"Home-y type?" I chuckle.

"Well, yeah. I pictured you in a mid-sized, one-bedroom apartment—not a massive home fit for ten," Eve replies.

"So, you thought about my living arrangements," I said more than asking.

"No. Yes, but that's not the point," Eve says, flustered.

"What is the point?" I lift an eyebrow.

"The point is, I didn't expect to end up here with you." Eve squinted her eyes at me while pursing her lips.

"But you are. So, let's do what we came to do." I stare at Eve for a long moment before taking a step toward her.

Eve holds her head high, refusing to back down from my taunt. "Let's do it." She says, feigning confidence.

I hook my finger around her pinkie. Then, I turn in the opposite direction, bringing Eve with me. She gives slight resistance as we walk but doesn't try to stop me. I know what I want to happen tonight, but I have to wonder about her. What does Eve want?

We walk through the kitchen, stopping at a closed door down the hallway. I turn to Eve, letting go of her hand and placing my hand on her arm.

"After you," I said, smirking her way.

Eve hesitates before wrapping her hand around the doorknob and turning it, easing the door open. She breathes deeply, staring into the darkness. "Do you expect me to go down there?" She asks.

"I expect nothing more than what you're comfortable with, Eve. I could go alone, but I think you'll like what you find down there."

"How do I turn on the lights?"

"You'll see once you're inside."

Eve looks at my hand on her arm, shrugging it away. Then, she takes the first step forward and another, pausing when the wall to her left begins to light her way. She glances over her shoulder at me and continues down the stairs. When we reach the bottom, she turns to her right, and a low gasp leaves her.

"I knew you would approve," I said proudly, staring at the oversized racks used to house my wine. A floor-to-ceiling shelf sits next to them, stocked with various spirits.

"Are you in the habit of hosting secret parties?" Eve asks. "Are you an alcoholic?" She looks at me, and I laugh.

"I'm a collector. It's a hobby of sorts," I answered. "So, what's your poison?" I walk to stand behind the bar, waiting for Eve's response.

Eve comes closer. A small smile is perched on her face. She stops on the other side of the bar, directly in front of me. "You're the expert. What do you think?"

"Hmm," I said, my eyes casually drifting over her. "From what I know of you, you prefer the light stuff—wine coolers and beer."

Eve quirks a smile. "True, but how did you come to that conclusion?" She flattens her palm on the bar.

"One word, Eve. Control. You have to have it. The light stuff provides pleasure without the fear of losing control." I touch the tip of my fingers to hers, capturing her gaze. Eve sucks in a breath, looking away. "I'm going to introduce you to the dark side tonight, Eve. If you want out, speak now."

Eve's eyes flit back to mine, and her cheeks flush. I held her gaze for a long moment before turning toward the wall to choose for her.

I pop the cork on a bottle of whiskey and half-fill two shot glasses. I balance the mini glasses between my fingers in my left hand while holding the bottle in the other as I walk back toward the bar.

"You've done this before," Eve implies.

I smirk. "Not here, and not with you."

"I guess that makes it all better," Eve says.

*That makes you special.*

I pass Eve on my way to the sofa, and she hesitates before she follows me. She sits as close to one end of the sofa as possible, trying to put space between us. I sat at the other end, grateful there wasn't another seating option in this area. There is a bedroom to our right with a plush ottoman at the foot, but I imagine Eve wants no part of that—net yet, at least. I free my hands, placing the contents on the table in front of us.

I stare at Eve, unable to pull my eyes away, and she stares back. Seconds tick by until she gives in and looks at the coffee table. She grabs the remote, aiming it at the seventy-two-inch flat screen and clicking the power button. I retrieve the remote from her hand and turn the tv off.

"What the hell, Devlin?" Eve asks.

"That's not what we're here to do." I set the remote down on the end of the table.

"Well, please enlighten me," Eve snaps, and fuck, I want her fire all over me.

I lean back on the sofa, placing my arm over the top. My eyes travel the length of her, and I clear my throat. "I can't believe I'm saying this, but let's talk."

"About what?" Eve eyes me suspiciously.

"Tell me about your ex. Why did you split?"

Eve gives me a skeptical look. "Seriously?"

"I want to know," I said truthfully. I'm anxious to know what John did to ruin a life with a good woman. I want to know so that I don't make the same mistake.

Eve picks up a glass from the table and downs it without thought. She slams the glass on the table, and her eyes widen. Her hand clutches her throat as she begins to cough. I hurry to get her a glass of tap water, returning quickly. She takes the glass, downing it in the same fashion as the whiskey.

I place my hand on Eve's knee to calm her, and it works like a charm. "You only get one more taste of water tonight. I'd suggest you sip slowly next time." I remove my hand from her knee, reclaiming my position on the sofa.

"Where were we?" Eve asks, scooting to the sofa's edge as if she's afraid to get comfortable.

"John," I remind Eve, turning her expression sour.

"Yeah, right." Eve clasps her hands on her lap. "John. We grew apart. Our relationship started great with minimal progression over the years. I guess we stopped trying along the way," Eve pauses, tilting her head to one side. "Are you sure you want to hear this?"

17

"You're my partner, Eve. We work closely. You were distracted today, and if this is the cause, I'd like to hear about it." A line has definitely been crossed, but I'm not turning back. We've skirted around each other for too long, and I doubt I'll have another chance to get close to her after tonight.

"I'm capable of figuring out my own mess, Devlin. I don't need you to analyze me. I have someone for that," Eve says curtly.

"Exactly. I'm not a therapist or a friend. I'm here to listen, not judge. I want you to get the shit off your chest so we can move on." I pause, shocked by my admission. "We're not an effective team if our minds are not focused."

Eve's eyes widen as her body shifts uncomfortably from one side to the other.

"Be honest," I continued. "You want an unbiased ear. That's why you agreed to spend the evening with me."

Eve huffs, picking up my glass and taking a sip. She sets the glass down and relaxes back onto the sofa. "Why do I feel like I'm going to regret this?" She mumbles. "Just remember you asked for it," she says, resting her head on the back of the sofa.

"I'm a great listener, among many other things," I told her.

Eve keeps her head back, staring at the ceiling as she begins talking. I take in every word for the next forty minutes, giving short responses in between. She manages to finish off another shot glass while sharing her story.

As Eve spoke, I watched her keenly and learned quite a few things. Her relationship with John was more of an arrangement than anything else. Sure, she's upset about their breakup, but I don't think it's because she lost the love of her life. I've concluded that John truly is an asshole. In his right mind, what man could restrain from sinking deep inside her even for a day, let alone an entire month? Eve has hips like a goddess, hips that I'd love to hold onto while fucking her.

I reach for the bottle on the table, pouring myself a glass since Eve took the last one. Her words are slow as she watches me bring the glass to my lips, letting the warm liquid slide down my throat. Being around her without the distraction of work is harder than I thought.

"So, what do you think?" Eve asks once I set the glass back down.

"I think you are worth so much more than him," I speak candidly. "And now that he's gone, you're free to do what you've always wanted, with whom you want to do it."

Eve's eyes drift over me as she takes a small sip from her glass and sets it back down. "I don't get it. Who are you right now?" she asks. "At work, you're this flirty, playful, intolerable woman's man, and here.... I'm just surprised we could sit and have a normal conversation aside from business."

"There's a lot you don't know about me, Eve." There are things that no one knows.

"Why are you single, Devlin?" Eve blurts out. "I mean, don't you get lonely? Don't you want someone to share all of this with?"

"I do when the time is right. I'm in no rush to settle for the wrong woman," I point out.

Eve frowns at my statement. "You think I rushed things with John?"

"I think you were afraid of the alternative."

Eve clears her throat and looks away. "Thank God for new beginnings, right."

"Right, indeed." I size Eve up for a moment, ensuring the booze hasn't taken her too far. "Come closer, Eve," I said, beckoning her with two fingers.

Eve looks around my home as if we aren't the only two people here. "To you?"

I chuckle. "Yes."

"Why?"

"Because you want to."

Eve hesitates for a moment, then slides to the sofa's center, touching her thigh to mine. She keeps her hands in her lap, fingers entwined. Nervous tension rolls off her, but she tries her best not to show it.

"Relax, Eve. Tonight, is all about you and what you want."

Eve's eyes snap to mine, longing, searching. "Do you think…."

I drop my hand to Eve's shoulder, and she stops speaking. "Do I think?" I raise a brow, holding her gaze, my thumb drawing thorough circles on her arm.

"Do you think I'm beautiful?" Eve drops her eyes a fraction in a moment of insecurity before looking back at me.

I clip her chin, brushing my thumb lightly over the small dip beneath her lip. I move in closer so that our noses barely touch. "If you were mine, Eve, there would be no reason to question your beauty or worth. My actions would be a constant reminder. You would melt each time my eyes roamed over you and shiver with every touch. You would be the center of my world regardless of whether I was the center of yours." I remain there for a moment, thinking of tasting her lips and deciding against it. "You're fucking beautiful, Eve, but you're not mine." I drop my hand and retreat, keeping my arm around her. "I think highly of you, Eve, and you should do the same. Never let a man or anyone else decide who you are."

"Devlin.".

"Yeah."

"Don't let it go to your head, but I like you just a tad bit right now," Eve says, pinching her fingers together.

Fuck, it went straight to my head.

# Chapter 3

**Evelyn**

I HADN'T EXPECTED Devlin to respond with such finesse. He said what I needed to hear, and if I didn't know him so well, I might have believed he meant every word. Instead, I'm choosing to accept them because I need this moment.

I lean into Devlin's side, soaking up his warmth as I stare into his eyes. I blame the alcohol for everything—liking his words, his touch, his attention, for wanting him as I do. He and I will never be friends or anything more. He's made that clear more than once tonight. What he's offering is *right now* out of pity, and I'm okay with that. We can go back to bickering when this is over. No ill feelings.

"Eve." Devlin holds my stare, his thumb still circling my shoulder. "It's getting late."

"Yes, it is," I agree.

"You have two choices," Devlin continues. "I could take you home, or we could do something about this tension." His eyes drop to my lips as his bottom lip dips into his mouth. Searing eyes find mine again, waiting for a response.

Devlin knew what he was doing when he brought me here. Sure, there's a choice, and I knew I had already decided the second I walked through his door. I never denied to myself the attraction I felt for Devlin. He's hot, but he's dangerous, hazardous to my health.

"I don't want to go home," I decided.

"Tell me what you want." Devlin lifts his hand to my lips, tracing them with his thumb.

"I want another drink."

"And?"

"You."

A satisfied smirk crosses Devlin's face as he studies me. "Don't worry, Eve. No one has to know."

I should be offended that he wants to keep me a secret, but I'm not. No one can know about this except the keeper of my secrets, Holland. I smile, hoping I don't regret this.

"I'm not worried. It's just one night." My chance to flush John completely out of my system. "I'm sure I'll forget all about it by morning. Nothing to tell," I tease, moving closer to Devlin's lips, but I'm met with two of his fingers pressed against my mouth.

"No kissing on the lips."

"Oh, okay." My brows furrow, and confusion and disappointment flow through me. I shouldn't be too surprised. Kissing is more intimate, and we are the furthest thing from it.

Devlin holds the left side of my neck in his hand and moves his head to the other side of my face, pressing his lips to my collarbone. He blows a cool breath over my skin, my eyes close, and my temperature rises in contrast. "Eve," he says barely above a whisper. His eyes are fiery when he pulls back to look at me.

Devlin smirks, putting a few inches between us. His hand moves to my thigh, slipping beneath my dress, and he grips tightly, guiding me to straddle him. His other hand holds my neck, and in one swift motion, he flips me onto the sofa, settling between my legs. I yelped at the sudden movement, my eyes going wide. Strong hands travel my thighs, inching my dress higher and landing on my ass with a gentle squeeze.

Being here with Devlin in this position is certainly different. My imagination has nothing on the real thing. My eyes drift toward the ceiling as his thumb traces the outline of my panties near my belly. I am ever grateful I didn't opt for grannies this morning.

"Eve." My eyes fall back on Devlin. "Watch while I take care of you." His command sends my heart racing in my chest. All I can do is nod my agreement.

Devlin's eyes drop, his head lowering to my chest. He pinches my nipple between his lips over the fabric of my dress, coaxing an unexpected moan from me. His kisses seep through my skin as he trails down my belly. Reaching the pulsing bud between my legs, he draws in a breath, releasing it on a low growl.

Devlin rises, one knee on the sofa, one foot on the floor, and pushes my dress over my hips. "Let's get naked, Eve."

While Devlin's words are blunt, they're also a complete turn-on. The way he commands and expects it's no surprise. Devlin isn't shy in the least at work. Why should his extracurricular activities be different? So, I sit up and do as he asks, stripping down to my underwear as he removes every inch of clothing from his body. My mouth waters at the sight of him before me. His ego is front and center, standing at attention. All of him, solid, hard muscle, calling out to me.

"I want to see all of you, Eve." Devlin glances at my bra and panties. Then, his eyes find mine again.

I'm not easily intimidated by Devlin, but we're not in the office anymore. I'm not used to anyone looking at me the way he is now. John was a lazy lover, me on top, lights off, just sex, no passion. He certainly never requested to look at me naked.

"Can't we just do it and get it over with?"

Devlin's eyes shrink to slits, his jaw ticking as he stares at me. "I don't know what you're used to, Eve, but this is not it. I want to see the product before testing. I give my best or nothing at all. If you're having second thoughts...."

"No," I said quickly. "Let's continue." I stand and remove my underwear, looking around, unsure what to do next.

Devlin takes me in, his eyes roaming over me, heating my skin. He drags his fingers down between my breast, and my nipples harden further. "You're beautiful, Eve," he says, his hand circling my breast as his lips clamp over it.

I grab Devlin's biceps, whimpering into his hair as he licks my other nipple, pulling it into his mouth. He releases my breast and grips my hips. His tongue trails the length of my belly as he kneels before me, leaving a mountain of need in its path.

"Devlin, what are you doing?" I ask, knowing but unbelieving. It's obvious what he's doing by the direction he's headed, but I can't fathom why he would want to go there with me. "No one's ever...." My mouth clamps shut, trapping my confession inside.

"All the more reason for me to continue," Devlin says, reading my mind. "I'm going to taste you, Eve, and you'll enjoy it."

"Your arrogance is showing, Devlin," I said breathily.

Devlin responds by lifting my right leg over his shoulder. He presses his thumb to my clit, then travels the entire length of me. He growls, his deep tone vibrating through me. "So wet already, Eve. Tell me it's all mine." He presses his thumb to me again, and I stifle a moan.

I'm as ready as I've ever been because of Devlin but reluctant to admit it out loud.

Devlin flicks his tongue over me once, twice, before pulling back. "Say it, Eve. This," he says, flicking again, "is mine."

My mind is scrambled, making it hard to think straight. Logically, I know that no part of me belongs to Devlin, but at this moment, all I want is to be claimed by him. "It's yours."

Devlin squeezes my thigh on his shoulder, pulling my bud into his mouth and sucking. My fingers slide into the hair at the back of his head, gripping it, drawing him closer. His name is on the tip of my tongue, but I swallow it. His thick tongue laps the length of me, his hand moving to my back. Within seconds, he flings my other leg over his shoulder, and I'm on the sofa with his head still in place. I can't help but think that I made the right choice. I'm dealing with a pro.

Devlin's head bobs between my thighs, tasting, teasing, torturous pleasure that has my back arching a short moment later. My body trembles around him, but he doesn't let up. His tongue dips inside me repeatedly until I collapse on the sofa.

Devlin raises his head to look at me. "So responsive," he says with a look of approval. "Tell me you want more." Something primal in his eyes pulls me in, causing my need for him to grow.

"More. I want more."

Devlin fists his shaft, pumping slowly, and I can't look away. He pulls a condom from his wallet and sheathes himself. He opens my legs wide, positioning himself at my center.

I lean forward, wrapping my arms around his neck as he eases the tip of his dick inside me. He pushes further inside, and I cry out softly, "Devlin," just as he grunts, "Eve. So wet. So tight. If I'm hurting you, tell me to stop," he whispers next to my ear. His voice is strained and his body rigid as if he's afraid of breaking me, but he's too far gone to stop.

"More," I breathe out.

Devlin continues. My legs press firmer to his sides the deeper he goes. He's bigger than I'm used to, stretching me as he moves forward. The feeling is both pleasurable and painful.

"Relax, Eve. Let me in." Devlin's tongue slides over my earlobe. His lips kiss the side of my neck and shoulder, and I obey, relaxing around him as much as possible. "That's it. Take all of me," he encourages.

"Dev…. Ah." My breath hitched as he sank himself to the hilt.

Devlin withdraws, leaving the tip inside. Then, plunges into me again. "Fuck," he groans, the pressure filling me again and again. Our movements sync, bodies conform as if we were meant to be one.

Devlin rises, bringing me with him. My arms are laced around his neck as he walks into the bedroom. Jolts of pressure pulsate against my wall as he moves. He eases out of me, setting me down on the bed. I stare at him, shocked by the loss, enamored with his girth. I swallow deeply, climbing further on the bed until I reach the pillows, and he climbs in after me. He pauses between my thighs, dipping his head to taste me again, teasing me with his tongue sliding over me and his finger massaging my clit.

"Devlin, please," I beg, gripping his hair and pressing my head into the pillow. I'm a proud lover, not one to beg, but he makes it hard not to. "I want you inside me. Now."

"Mmm," Devlin hums over my skin. He lifts his head, positioning himself over me.

My mouth waters, my body craving his touch. I'm too far gone. I know it because I want to kiss him, despite the rule.

Devlin licks his lip as if reading my mind. Then he dives inside me again, keeping his eyes on mine. The feel of his dick sliding in and out of me, coupled with the intensity of his gaze, is too much at once. I close my eyes, shake away our thoughts and focus on the sex.

The headboard creeks under Devlin's grip as he pounds into me. He grabs my waist, burying his head in the crook of my neck. My body quakes moments later as he pulses inside me, grunting into my ear. Sweat drips from his forehead as he pulls away to lay beside me. He discards the condom, and minutes pass with us staring at the ceiling in silence.

My thoughts are rampant, unrealistic, daring even.

*Devlin is not such a bad guy.*

*That was the best sex I've ever had.*

*I could get used to this.*

And one very sobering thought.

*I just had sex with Devlin, my coworker whom I swore would never get close.*

# Chapter 4

**Devlin**

I LOOK AT EVE lying next to me, bathing in the afterglow. She hasn't spoken since we finished, and neither have I. She was perfect and fit me like a glove after working my way in. I didn't expect to want more so soon. I glance at her lips, silently cursing myself for the rule. I can't catch feelings for her. She clarified that this was not a date when I picked her up. It's just a hookup between consenting adults—between coworkers. It probably wasn't the best idea, but Eve had that look like she wanted to forget. I wanted to be the one who took her away.

I cross my hands behind my head on the pillow, my head in her direction and body still on display. I smirk at the thought in my mind, knowing it will push her buttons and not caring.

"No offense, Eve." Her head jerks toward me. "But John didn't know what the fuck he was doing."

Eve's eyes widen, and she braces on her elbows, her nipples pert, chest heaving. "How dare you? You don't know shit about my relationship," she snaps.

"You mean the one that ended?" I lift a brow.

Eve opens her mouth and closes it just as quickly.

"If he did, you'd be in his bed instead of mine. He wasn't man enough for you. You deserve better."

"And you're better?"

I consider Eve's question. I may not be the best man for her, but I am better than her ex. "I'm just a man, Eve. But I know an unsatisfied woman when I see one. Tell me. How do you feel?"

Eve swallows, her eyes turning to slits as she glares at me. "You're an arrogant asshole."

I look at the ceiling, chuckling. "That may be, but you wanted me. You enjoyed it, and you're sated." I enjoyed her as well, maybe too much.

Eve sits up, attempting to get out of bed, but I grab her wrist before she can escape. "Where are you going?"

Eve's head swings toward me. "Home."

"Stay. Get some rest. I'll take you home in the morning."

Eve stares at me for a few seconds, unmoving.

"Look, I shouldn't have said those things." Though, I meant every word. I want her to stay. I'm not ready to go back to the way we were yet. It's nice having her in my bed, my space, period.

Eve looks at my hand on her wrist, and I drop it.

"Stay. I'll be on my best behavior tonight."

Eve considers my offer, her features softening. "I'll stay, but only because I'm tired and don't know where I am."

"You're safe here with me. Now lay that pretty head on my pillow and go to sleep."

Eve protests, remaining where she is for seconds longer before getting under the covers and lying down. She huffs, then turns her back to me.

I smile, joining her beneath the sheets, but keeping to my side. "Good night, Eve."

"Good night, Devil."

I smile as her visible cheek rises to meet her eyes.

I OPEN MY EYES, trying to adjust to the dim lighting in the basement. It's my first time sleeping down here. My first time waking up to a woman's head lying on my chest and leg draped over my thighs.

The events of last night came rushing back to me in a flash. My arm is wrapped loosely around Eve as if this is normal for us. It's not normal, but it feels right. I never imagined falling for any woman, but I'd make an exception for Eve if she allowed it. Last night was amazing, and the fact that she'll never be mine made it better. I played on her grief, and she knew it, but it was worth having her for one night to wake up to her this morning. We used each other.

"Mmm," Eve stirs, her hips rocking against my side. "Yes. Right there," she mumbles. Her thigh presses into mine, toes digging into my shin. "Yes," she moans breathily.

My body stills, giving her free reign to continue. I want to join in, and at the same time, I want to watch her fall apart without me.

Eve's hand moved down my chest, settling around my cock. I stay still as her hand rises and falls over me, her hip following the motion. My dick thickens in her grasp. I should stop her, but I can't. It's sexy as fuck, her moans, her touch, her warm breath coating my skin, asking for more. I wonder if it's my face she sees inside her head. No woman has ever made me come by her hands alone, but I'm on the brink of letting go.

"It's yours," Eve says. "Take it."

I give in to the feeling, imagining filling her as she grips and slacks around me over and over again. Eve's hand moves faster. The buildup is quick, and I jerk my hips in her hand, ejaculating onto my chest, scarcely escaping her face. "Eve." Her name leaves my mouth so softly that I barely recognize my voice. What is this woman doing to me?

My arm tightens around Eve, and her eyes pop open. She lifts her eyes to mine, jerking her hand away from me. "What the hell did you do?"

My brows lift. "I was just about to ask you the same question." I glance at the mess I made and back at her. "Thanks for that, by the way. Perfect start to my morning." I smirk.

Eve looks horrified. She removes herself from my hold, scooting to her side of the bed. "Take me home," she demands. She gives me a look that could kill.

"I would much rather talk about what just happened."

"Nothing happened. I was asleep." She pulls the sheet over her breast.

"I know. You acted out your dream on me, which was surprising, by the way. But I'm glad to be of service."

"Why did you? Why didn't you wake me?"

I grin. "My mother told me never to wake an active dreamer. You could've killed me." I feign innocence. "I was also told that dreams house our hearts' desires. Do you think that's true, Eve?"

"You're an ass…."

"Hole, I know," I finished her sentence.

"I never should've come with you."

Her words sting, but I don't let the hurt show. "We did a lot more than *come* together, Eve."

"That's it. Home. Now." Eve turns away from me, throwing her legs over the bed and standing. "This will never happen again," she fumes.

I get up, following Eve out of the bedroom, where she gathers her clothes and puts them on. I still don't want her to leave, but my experience with her has taught me a few things. Eve can dish it as well as she can take it, but even she has a breaking point. When she's truly adamant about something, there's no changing her mind. Playtime is over.

I wipe away the evidence of the last few minutes in the bathroom and slip on my clothes from the night before since all my things are upstairs. Eve waits impatiently, tapping her feet at the top of the stairs with her arms crossed over her chest.

I climb the stairs, closing the door once I reach the top. "Let's get you home, Princess." I walk past Eve and out the garage door. She closes the door behind us and gets into the passenger seat of my car.

The drive to Eve's place is quiet. She keeps her eyes open this time, taking stock of her surroundings. I take my time, still not ready to let go of her.

Pushing Eve's buttons has always been one of my favorite pass times. Gauging her posture and how she refuses to look at me now, I may have gone too far this time.

I continue through the city limits to the opposite side of town, where Eve lives. Her hand is on the doorknob before the car makes a complete stop.

"What's the rush?" I ask, glancing at her.

Eve forces a smile. "I've got things to do today."

I park the car in her driveway, dropping my arm to the armrest and turning slightly toward her. "Really?" I'm intrigued. "What's a woman like you do when she's not at work by your lonesome?" I haven't pictured her doing anything but work since we met. Mostly because I hated imagining her with John.

"A woman like me keeps men like you out of her business. Now, if you'll excuse me." Eve pulls the latch on the car door, and it clicks open.

"Wait." I grab her arm, and she pauses, looking my way again. "I enjoyed this time with you, Eve." My brows furrow, confused by my words. That's not what I had expected to say. I'm usually cautious about letting anyone see my vulnerability.

Eve stares, her eyes dropping to my lips before returning to mine. "Don't say that. You don't have to pretend this was more than what it was. I'm a big girl. You're a big boy." Eve swallows deeply as if remembering something. "We fucked. End of story. It's not complicated. See you at work Monday." Eve opens the door fully, drawing her body away from my hold, and gets out, closing it behind her.

I put the window down, refusing to let her have the last word. "Eve. If you ever need another *drink*, I'm your number one." I put the window up and back out of the driveway, leaving Eve standing there gazing as I pull away.

# Chapter 5

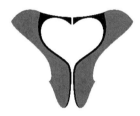

**Evelyn**

"YOU'RE LUCKY I'M currently between flings." Holland pops an M&M into his mouth as he steps inside my home. "Or your desperate plea would've gone unanswered." He walks straight to the fridge, and I close the front door, following behind him.

"You're such a loyal best friend," I responded, sarcasm dripping from my tongue. I smile with satisfaction, admiring Holland. We have been best friends since middle school. He is shy of six feet, has a slim build, with a great personality. People have often mistaken us for a couple, but that's not the kind of connection we have. He's too neat for me. Don't get me wrong. It's an appealing quality, but not for me.

41

"What's so urgent that you dragged me over here before nine on a Saturday?" Holland eyes me curiously.

My elbow rests in my hand with my fist on my chin. "I think I made a huge mistake." I walk out of the kitchen and into the living room, hearing Holland's footsteps close behind me.

"You can't drop a line like that and walk away, Eve."

I roll my eyes and plop down on the center of the couch.

Holland sits next to me with a can of Sprite in one hand and M&Ms in the other. He pops one into his mouth, speaking around the crunch. "Is this about John?"

Holland has opinions about John, as any best friend would, but he never got in the way of us. He neither encouraged nor discouraged my breakup. He pointed out the pros and cons and left me to weigh my options. That's why I love him and why John didn't feel threatened by him.

I cut my eyes at Holland, sure that what I was about to tell him would come as a complete shock. "It's so far beyond John."

Holland's brows bunch as he pops the last M&M into his mouth. "You're predictable, Eve. What could be beyond John?"

"I slept with Devlin." The words are out of my mouth before I can think about it.

Holland respects me, but in this instance, I expect a shameful comment that tells me I was wrong. His mouth falls open, and I wait.

And wait.

And wait.

I turn to face Holland on the couch. He appears completely stunned, speechless. "Say something." I nudge his leg with my knee.

"Well, shit." Holland stares at me. "I didn't see that one coming." He opens his can and downs the soda, setting the remnants on the coffee table.

Holland has seen Devlin before, but they've never met. He also knows that Devlin is the last person I'd be caught dead with out of the office.

"Neither did I." I glanced away momentarily, feeling ashamed.

"To be clear, your co-worker, Devlin?" Holland asks.

"Yes."

"But you said that would never happen."

I shrug. "Well, apparently, I'm not so predictable anymore, and clearly, my judgment left with John."

"So, what happens now?"

"Nothing. I made it clear to Devlin that we would never do *it* again."

Holland stares at me skeptically but doesn't comment.

"You think I'm a slut," I sigh, fiddling with the hem of the shorts I'd changed into after Devlin dropped me off.

Holland chuckles. "I don't think you're a slut. I think you wanted to get laid. You wanted to forget John and aren't ready for another relationship. So, naturally, you turned to a guy you know can't commit. That doesn't make you a bad person."

"Why do I feel like I've committed the greatest sin?"

"Because you did," Holland raised a brow.

My jaw drops. "Holland." I throw a light punch at his chest.

"What?" He grunted out over a laugh.

"Just for that, I should tell you all about it." I wiggle my brows.

"Please spare me the details. I can't think of you that way with any man."

I laugh. Discussing my sexcapades is a hard limit for Holland. He says as much each time I threaten to enlighten him. He has no issues telling me about his before, now, and after, though, and I don't mind hearing it. Until I met John, I had lived vicariously through Holland and even more so afterward. Our sex life was sporadic, sometimes planned. But last night with Devlin was like a chapter from Holland's book. I felt alive for the first time in forever.

I close my eyes, remembering Devlin's touch. His muscles rippled beneath his skin. His deep growls and thick ...."

"Damn," Holland says.

My eyes snap open. "What?"

"I don't want to hear about it, but I give the guy props for leaving a lasting impression."

"It will be out of my system soon enough," I said, owning up to Holland's implication. There's no use denying it when it comes to him. He knows all of my quirks, expressions, and body language.

"By Monday?" Holland questions.

"I'm sure I'll be fine once Devlin opens his mouth." I smile, hoping my words are bond.

"For your sake, I hope that's true." Holland doesn't seem convinced.

I'm not convinced, either. Devlin set the bar high. He gave me an experience I've never had. One that I won't soon forget.

"You're doing it again," Holland says.

"Ugh," I groaned in frustration.

Holland looks around the house. "What are your plans now that John is gone?"

I follow his movements, grateful for the change in topic. "I hadn't thought about it."

John and I bought the place as a starter home, hoping to get married and fill it with two or three kids one day. The marriage never happened, and the kids, well, it was never the right time. There were no ties between us when he left since everything was in my name, and thankfully so.

"I could sell it and move in with you," I suggest.

Holland shakes his head in protest. "I love you, Eve, but your suggestion is cause for disaster. The only woman I'll ever live with is *The One*, and maybe my mother. I can't have you falling for me because you like how my boxers frame my ass," he jokes.

I cough out a laugh. "I've seen you in your boxers before, Holland. Pretty sure I didn't fall for you."

"I was thirteen, Eve. Besides, everyone knows that proximity and longevity heighten feelings. So, it could go one of two ways. Either we'll love each other more or hate each other's guts in the end. I'd rather not chance it."

"So, you'd leave me hanging?"

"No. I would do everything I can to help you find a good roommate if that's what you want. It just can't be me. I value our friendship too much."

"I respect that," I told Holland. "Guess I'll hang on to this place longer then."

"I know what you need." Holland rubs his chin between his middle and pointer fingers.

I cock my head in interest, thinking *another hit of Devlin.* "What do you have in mind?"

"Get dressed. We're going out."

# Chapter 6

**Devlin**

THERE WAS A difference in the atmosphere when I got back home. It's colder and less filling. I've lived here for six years and never brought a woman home until last night. I want to regret my choice, but I don't feel it was a mistake.

I walk down into the basement, pausing at the base of the stairs for a moment. I put the whiskey bottle away and cleaned the empty glasses. I change the sheets, remake the bed, and pull the small bag from the trash bin in the bedroom. Even so, Eve still lingers.

Last night was incredible. I'm not sure how I'll be able to face Eve again without wanting to touch her or remembering her taste on my lips.

The doorbell sounds as I reach the top of the stairs, and I answer it. The door is pushed open the second the hinge clicks, knocking my hand away.

"Why are you here, Vicky?" My eyes follow Victoria as she walks past me without an invite. Her hand flings over her shoulder, disregarding me. I shake my head, close the door, and follow her. "Vicky," I said again.

Victoria is my younger sister, who just began her first year at West Lake University a few months ago. I'm sixteen years her senior, but she acts like she's older and in charge. Until a few years ago, we barely talked due to our age difference. Vicky took the initiative to get to know me better. Rather than push her away, I let her in. I only regret my decision when she shows up like today—unannounced.

"What?" Vicky swings around, propping her hands on her hips. "I came to see you."

"Really? Because you walked past me with barely a glance. Were you expecting someone else? Some kind of excitement?"

"Well, no. But I had hoped." She drops one arm to her side, sighing. "You live like a bachelor, Dev."

I chuckle, stepping closer and stopping inches away. "I am a bachelor. Shouldn't you be studying or partying? Whatever kids your age do."

"First," Vicky ticks off a finger. "I'm not a kid. I'm eighteen. Second," she ticks off another finger. "The party's not until tonight. And third," she wiggles three fingers in the air. "It's the weekend, and I don't need to study."

"Don't you have friends you could hound?"

"I do, but I need a favor." Vicky smiles innocently.

"A favor from *me*?" I cross my arms over my chest.

"Yes, from the best big brother in the whole wide world." Vicky pauses, her eyes dropping to the small bag in my hand. "Why are you holding an empty trash bag?"

I had forgotten the bag was there. The evidence would've been discarded if Vicky hadn't popped up. I hold the bag steady, trying to remain normal, unbothered. I tilt my head, staring her down. "What's the favor?" I asked, disregarding her question.

Vicky glances at the bag again, then back at me. "I have a project that would require my tagging along with you to work for a day."

"Why didn't you ask Dad?"

"You're kidding, right?" Vicky asks incredulously. "Dad is not the right man for the job, and you know it. He'd have me scrubbing floors and fetching his lunch just for the hell of it." She scrunches her nose. "You have to help me," she says, pressing her palms together.

Vicky's project must be important. She doesn't beg me for anything. She demands. Though, it's understandable why she didn't ask our father, given his inability to connect with anyone but himself. He's always been harder on Vicky and me than anyone else. I hated him as a child, mostly because I didn't know or understand him. I understand all I need to know now. My father is a provider, but he's shit at relationships. I guess I'm sort of like him in that way, and I mean that lightly. My needs are met, and I can connect just fine, but I'm only committed to my job. I like my life on-axis. So, I stay clear of anything or anyone that threatens that. At least until Eve.

"I guess I could help you out."

Vicky rushes over, her small frame crashing into mine as she throws her arms around my back, knocking the breath out of me. "Thank you. Thank you. Thank you." She releases me, stepping away to recompose herself.

I rarely see Vicky disheveled. She didn't have the childhood that most kids have, and neither did I. We were expected to be poised at all times, where my father was concerned. If it weren't for Mom, I wouldn't have known what play was. And if it weren't for college, Vicky would still be held captive.

"Don't thank me yet." I grin. "You can tag along, but I won't show favoritism. There's work to be done, and I will ensure you earn your grade."

"Yes, Sir," Vicky said, saluting me. "I promise. I won't cause trouble."

"When do we do this?" I ask, turning and walking toward the garage door. I'm starting to feel uncomfortable with a bag full of semen in my sister's company.

"Monday," Vicky yells after me.

I open the door and step into the garage long enough to throw the bag into the huge bin. Vicky is headfirst in my fridge when I get back. "That doesn't leave much time to prepare," I told her.

"What's there to prepare for?" Vicky stands straight, giving me a corner glance before looking back inside the fridge. "I've been prepped all of my life. Whatever you need me to do, I'll do it." She closes the fridge.

I lean against the sink next to her. Vicky's presence at work could prove to be a good thing for both of us. I could introduce her to Eve and let her pry and feel things out. "Be there by eight. No excuses. Or the deals off."

"Eight PM. Got it," Vicky says, smiling.

"I'm serious, Vicky. Don't be late."

"I know. I know. Geez. Lighten up, will you?" Vicky huffs, pointing her finger at the fridge. "You realize there's nothing in there to eat, right?"

I raise my brows. "Just because it's not what you want doesn't mean there's nothing there."

Vicky waves my comment away. "You're taking me out for breakfast," she says, back to her demanding ways, gaining a laugh from me.

Vicky makes herself comfortable while I get dressed. I'm not too fond of her pop-up visits, but it's hard to say no to her. She's the only real family I have left, and I love her.

Ten minutes later, Vicky and I are going to Brecks Bagels. She lectures me the entire ride about women and how she thinks I should have one and only one for the rest of my life. She wants a fairy tale, but I don't believe in that kind of life. Sure, I want to be married someday. But, I'm not naive to think it will be perfect because I'm far from it. Mistakes will be made. Hearts will be broken. That's what I believe.

"Are you listening to me?" Vicky asks as I park in the side lot of Brecks.

"I heard every word." I pull the keys out of the ignition.

"But did you *hear* me?"

"Let's go inside." I ignore Vicky, opening my door and getting out, and she follows.

"You know I'm right," Vicky says as we trek down the sidewalk.

I give her a side hug, glancing her way. "It will happen, Vicky, when the time is right."

Vicky smiles wide. "I'll table it for now, but this conversation is not over."

I chuckle, looking ahead as we near the entrance. I stop suddenly, my hand on Vicky's shoulder, halting her along with me.

"Why did we stop? Is something wrong?" Vicky asks.

"No." I cleared my throat, eyes focused on the woman standing before us.

*Eve.*

Eve stares at me, mouth wide, and my eyes roam over her. She's wearing blue slim-fit jeans and a white shirt—a stark change from her normal attire. She looks comfortable but still every bit as beautiful as always. I like it.

"Devlin," Eve says, appearing shocked to see me. "What are you doing here?"

I give her a half-smile, amused by how flustered she is. "I was about to ask you the same thing."

Eve's eyes flit to Vicky and back to mine. She flashes a white paper bag between us and lifts the carrier in her other hand with two cups nestled inside. "Breakfast," She offers as an excuse.

"All for you?" I ask, glancing at the carrier.

"Yes. No," Eve grins, shaking her head. "For a friend."

I dropped her off only a short while ago. I stare curiously at Eve, wondering who her friend is. Will she tell them about last night? Are they really a friend or another hookup? I'd hate for it to be the latter.

"Ahem," Vicky clears her throat next to me. I pull my eyes away from Eve to look at her. "Aren't you going to introduce me to your friend?" She asks.

"We aren't friends," Eve says quickly, drawing my attention back to her. "We're coworkers." She glances at my arm around Vicky, a momentary frown appearing on her face.

My brows tweak. "Right," I agreed sarcastically. We may not be friends, but we're much more than coworkers after last night. We crossed a line that will be hard to move on from. My arm falls from Vicky's shoulder, gesturing to Eve. "This is Evelyn. My *coworker*," I said to Vicky. "Evelyn, this is my...."

"I'm Victoria," Vicky says, cutting me off. "It's a pleasure finally meeting one of Dev's acquaintances."

"Pleasure to meet you too," Eve responds with a forced smile. She looks at me, squinting her eyes in annoyance. "I should be going. See you at work Monday, *Dev*," Eve says snippily. Then she steps around us, heading in the opposite direction. I look over my shoulder, watching her walk away.

"See you soon, Evelyn," Vicky calls after her.

I swallow deeply, then turn back in the direction Vicky and I were headed. "Come on." I direct Vicky to the entrance of Brecks, open the door, and step inside. We stop behind a woman in line, and I can feel Vicky's gaze burning the side of my face. I sense the many questions floating inside her head when I look at her—questions I'm not prepared to answer.

"What was that about?" Vicky asks.

"What?" I cross an arm over my belly, resting my elbow on top and pinching my chin.

"You and Evelyn seem like more than coworkers," Vicky says, stating the obvious. "And she's a beauty."

"Well, we're not," I lied.

"What's stopping you?" Vicky smiles as the woman in front of us looks over her shoulder and turns back around.

"It's complicated." Much more complicated than I'm willing to share with my little sister.

"You shouldn't let a little thing like working together stop you from pursuing her. She could be the one. Didn't you notice her annoyance at how close we were?" Vicky asks.

"I did." I noticed and was turned on by Eve's actions, but I don't get why she'd be upset. She made it clear she didn't want me. "That wasn't cool, by the way, letting Eve think we were together."

"I did no such thing, but lucky for you; it got a rise out of her. You're welcome," Vicky says proudly.

The woman in front of us scowls as she walks away with her order, gaining a laugh from Vicky and me.

# Chapter 7

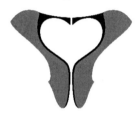

**Evelyn**

I BEHAVED LIKE a jealous ex on Saturday, but Devlin will never know the extent of my embarrassment or anger. I've spent hours over the past day and a half wondering how he could move on to someone else so quickly after the night we shared. But in hindsight, I can't blame him. He didn't make any promises. He never claimed to be anyone but who he is, and I claimed to care less.

I hate him.

I like him.

My feelings don't matter because Devlin is not the man for me, regardless of how his touch brought me to life. I've been dreading the face-off and wanting it all the same.

"It doesn't matter," I whisper as I exit my office to grab a coffee. I walk a few feet to the breakroom and pour myself a cup, adding two sugar packets and two creamers. I stir it with a short straw, then snap the top on, dipping the straw back inside. I take a sip, still facing the countertop, trying to focus on the day ahead.

"Good, you're here." Devlin's smooth voice travels through the room, causing me to jump and nearly drop my cup.

I turn to face him and almost drop the cup again. He stops inches away from me. "Don't sneak up on me like that, Devlin," I demand, frustration dripping from my words.

"Good morning to you too," Devlin responds.

"It was until you entered the room," I quipped with a snide smile.

Devlin smirks, and for a moment, I think he's going to bring up what happened between us, but he doesn't. "Mr. Sawyer called a meeting at 8:10 in the conference room."

I balk at the timing. "But that's in," I glance at my cell phone, "thirteen minutes."

Devlin nods, stepping around me to fix himself a cup of coffee. "Just thought I'd let you know."

I turn to face his back. "Any idea what it's about?"

Devlin snaps the top onto his cup and grabs a straw. "No. He didn't say." He turns, staring at me for a long moment, and I try to shelter any indications that it's affecting me. "I

60

have to meet my shadow in the lobby, but I'll see you there," he says before walking away.

It's just like normal, Devlin and me. Business as usual. Maybe I was worrying too much about seeing him again. He's acting like nothing ever happened between us, as promised, as I had hoped. It sort of hurts that he's so heartless, though.

*And what the hell did he mean by his shadow?*

I discard the thought, returning to my office to grab a pen and notepad. Then, I go to the conference room. I'm the first to arrive, thankfully. I sit in my usual chair, two spots away from Mr. Sawyer's right, so I appear eager but not the teacher's pet. Devlin usually sits next to me, in chair one.

Charity, Mr. Sawyer's favorite employee, is the second to enter the room. She takes chair one on the opposite side of the table. The moment she walks in, I know what the meeting is about.

Every year MS Toys picks one employee to co-host the annual Christmas Party. Thanks to Charity, I've volunteered three years in a row, but I've never been chosen. It's only speculation, but I suspect something is happening between Mr. Sawyer and her. Charity was always Mr. Sawyer's first choice and star employee of the few of us who volunteered. After years of trying, the rest of the faithful few gave up, all but me. I refuse to give up trying.

When I first learned of the opportunity, it was all about

the bonus and the possibility of being Mr. Sawyer's right hand that came along with it. Don't get me wrong. It's still about those things, but now it's more about the principle. I want to know that I'm valued, not because I'm chummy with the boss, but for my worth and what I bring to the table.

I look at Charity, painting a smile at the thought, and she smiles back. She's nice enough and pretty, showing a small glimpse of cleavage. I wish she would rely more on her smarts than her body.

I look up when Devlin walks in, and our eyes lock for a moment. Then, I noticed the woman from Saturday close behind him. The smile that had been forming quickly disappeared.

"Eve, you remember Victoria, right?" Devlin says, directing her to the chair next to Charity.

I nod. "Good to see you again."

"Vicky, this is Charity, manager of our design team—some of whom you'll meet shortly." Devlin pulls the chair out for her, and she sits, smiling brightly at him.

"Thanks, Dev," Victoria says, then looks at Charity. "Nice to meet you, Charity."

"You as well," Charity says.

Charity and Vicky shake hands, and all I can do is stare. I've never been so confused or bothered. Why is she here sitting across the table from me?

My eyes follow Devlin as he rounds the table and sits.

He doesn't explain, and I don't ask for an explanation. It's none of my business whom he screws and brings to work. I clear my throat, straightening in my chair as six additional employees enter the room and sit around the rectangular table.

"Team, this is Victoria. She's my shadow for the day," Devlin says to everyone around the table.

I force another smile, unsatisfied with Devlin's announcement. It sort of explains why Victoria is here, but not why they were together Saturday outside of work. I release a calming breath, reminding myself that it doesn't concern me. One night with him doesn't entitle me to know everything about him. But I feel entitled and hate the emotions coursing through me and the heat in my veins.

Mr. Sawyer is the last to enter, greeting everyone with a nod. His eyes fall on Charity, then skirt to Victoria. "Victoria. Glad you could join us. I hope you'll benefit from your time here today," he says.

I tilt my head slightly, wondering *what is going on.* Victoria's presence here was obviously planned if Mr. Sawyer knew. So, why didn't Devlin let me in on the secret? We're supposed to be partners unless he was trying to get under my skin.

I glance at Devlin, who is watching me.

*Was that your intention?* I silently asked Devlin.

I pull my eyes away from Devlin, giving my full

attention to Mr. Sawyer. I will not let Devlin rattle me. I can feel his eyes on me as Mr. Sawyer sits, but I ignore him.

"As you all know, the annual Christmas party is swiftly approaching," Mr. Sawyer begins, and Devlin turns to look at him. "The old rules still apply. If you would like to be considered, submit a theme, plan, and budget by the end of the week. The chosen will have one month to coordinate following the decision."

I glance at Charity, noticing a confident smile like she knows she's already won. I want to wipe that smile off of her face.

I look away from Charity, feeling a little guilty. I twist my pen between my fingers, completely distracted. Maybe I'm being unfair to her. Maybe her ideas are simply better than mine. I'm just as biased as the next person, thinking my work is the best, but I could be wrong. That doesn't stop me from wanting to come out on top, though.

"Evelyn," Mr. Sawyer draws my attention.

My eyes flit to his. "Yes, Mr. Sawyer?"

"Where are we on the Egg Project?"

*The infamous Egg Project.*

Every eye in the room is on me. I glance at Devlin, hoping he will chime in like he always does, but he remains quiet.

Mr. Sawyer threw the Egg Project onto Devlin and my plate about two weeks ago, and we've been skirting around it ever since, trying to decide if it's a marketable item. Someone pitched the bright idea of interactive Christmas eggs for kids. Eggs are usually reserved for Easter, but it deserves consideration because it's different. We're just not completely sold on the concept.

"It's still in beta testing," I responded. "We should have a decision by the end of the week." I glance at Devlin, and he nods his approval.

"Great," Mr. Sawyer says. "Does anyone else have anything new to report?" He asks the team.

An employee at the far end of the table speaks up, but I don't hear a word. I zone out as my eyes lock with Delvin's. There's something unfamiliar in his gaze—something new and questioning. Something that I realize is wrong, especially with his woman of the hour sitting across the table from me.

I look away, my eyes traveling to Victoria, watching us with fascination. I wonder if he's told her about us? She seems more intrigued than jealous. She smiles at me, much as she'd done when we first met, and I smile back at her.

Devlin slides a note over to me, and I look down to read it.

*"You're distracted again, Eve."*

The audacity. I can't look at Devlin. The last time I was distracted at work, I ended up in his bed. I straighten in my chair, pretending he and Victoria are not in the room. I tuned all the way into the meeting because that could not happen again.

# Chapter 8

**Devlin**

EVE HAS BEEN avoiding me since the meeting this morning. Vicky was right. Eve is jealous or pissed because she thinks I moved on quickly. I know it has everything to do with Vicky being here, whether she wants to admit it or not.

I admire Eve quietly from her open door for a few seconds before entering. She's either ignoring me or is hard at work with her eyes focused on the contents of the red folder on her desk.

I stop directly in front, opening my mouth to speak and effectively being cut off by Eve.

"What do you want, Devlin?" Eve asks, annoyed. Her head rises slowly, eyes lifting to meet mine. "I'm working, which leaves little time for me to entertain you."

I take it as an invitation and sit before her. My eyes fall to the folder on her desk that I've deemed her portfolio of possibilities. Eve has been hoping for a chance to host the company party for a while now, but she's always out-witted by Charity.

Eve clears her throat, drawing my eyes back to hers. "Since you obviously didn't understand me the first time, what do you want?" She repeats, plain and clear.

"I see you're diving into the den again." I nodded to the folder beneath her palms.

"And I see you still believe my business is yours." Eve quips.

"Well, one might argue that we are on the same team, and these are business hours, last I checked. That makes me privy to any projects you may be working on." I hold Eve's glare, smirking into it.

"Would it kill you to let me be for one day—to show some respect?" Eve questions.

I relax onto the cushion, resting my arms on the arms of the chair and pulling one leg up with my ankle perched atop my knee.

"Respect," I pause, allowing my eyes to roam over every visible part of Eve. "I respect you more than you know, more than you care to think about."

Eve's palms press harder to the folder as she swallows deeply. "I think we should keep our distance for a while."

"And I think we should do the opposite. Unless you want to be the topic of speculation." I raise an eyebrow.

"What do you want from me, Devlin?" Eve's eyes draw me in, her question throwing up red flags that I choose to ignore.

"I want my bickering buddy back. I thought we both agreed this wouldn't be awkward. It was just se...."

"Don't say it," Eve says quickly.

"Unless...." I tilt my head slightly, examining her expressions, feeling for the truth I want.

"No. You're right. That's all it was." Eve leans away from the desk, repositioning her body in the chair.

I'm a little disappointed by her response. I'm not sure if I'll ever be able to give Eve what she deserves, but I wish she had answered differently. I wish she had said that what we shared was more.

"Good because I came to ask you to lunch."

Eve blanches at my suggestion. "What?"

"Lunch. You haven't eaten, and neither have I. I thought we could do it together."

"You and me?" Eve questions.

I shrug. Vicky insisted I ask Eve to tag along with us. It's not the best idea she's ever had, but it's also not the worst.

Eve's eyes flash up toward the door leaving my question unanswered. An expression I can't decipher dawns on her face.

"Knock, knock," Vicky's voice sings throughout the office. She scrolls inside as if invited and stops next to me, placing her hand on my shoulder. "Good to see you again, Evelyn," she says, smiling. "Sorry to interrupt. I've been told I have boundary issues," she snickers. "Did you get around to asking her?" Vicky asks, looking at me expectantly while bumping her hip to my arm. When I don't answer immediately, she continues. "Men," she directs to Eve. "Dev was supposed to invite you to lunch."

"I did, and Eve was just about to…."

"Sure," Eve blurts out over a pasted smile. "I would love to join you," she says, piquing my interest.

Well, that took a turn I didn't expect. I was sure Eve would decline once she found out Vicky was going.

"Then, it's settled," Vicky chimes. "And it's Dev's treat."

My eyes meet Eve's briefly before she looks away.

"Even better," Eve agrees. Though, she doesn't seem too happy with me doing something else for her. I can see straight through her facade. She has to know that I don't expect anything from her—no more than she's freely willing to give. I may have a reputation for attracting women, but none of them have ever accused me of not being a gentleman.

EVE'S EYES MET mine quite a few times in my rearview on the ride to Phil's Diner. And each time, she would look away. Vicky offered her dibs at the front seat, but she declined, opting for the back. I suppose she may regret her decision, given that neither of us could resist the urge to steal glances along the way.

As soon as we arrive at Phil's and exit the car, Vicky links her arm through Eve's as if they're best friends and starts toward the entrance. Vicky talks a mile per minute while Eve looks ahead. I don't know why but the two of them together agree with me and bring a smile to my face.

Once we're inside and seated with Vicky next to Eve and me across the table, we place our order, and the server promptly brings our drinks. There's too much silence between us, the tension so thick I can cut it with a knife. I try, but I can't look away from Eve, and she refuses to look away from me.

"So, Eve." Vicky clears her throat, breaking Eve's eyes from mine. "What's it like working with this guy day in and day out?"

Eve entwines her fingers on the table, a slight smile gracing her lips. Her glance tells me she wants to spill the beans just to get under my skin, but she's a lady who never reveals her escapades to anyone.

"There's never a dull moment," Eve says. "Devlin has kept me on my toes from the moment we met. Challenge has been our strongest suit. I guess you could say we make a great team." She glances at me for a moment, a flash of softness in her eyes. Then she lifts her glass, pressing her lips around her straw, and sips her water.

Vicky glances at me with a devious gleam before turning her attention back to Eve. She leans forward a fraction, whispering over the table. "Have you two ever bumped bods?"

Eve's eyes go wide, water spurting from her mouth. She quickly sets the glass on the table, careful not to look at me. Her cheeks turn a shade darker as she rushes to grab a few napkins, dabbing at her mouth and dress.

I'm shocked that Vicky would be so bold. I'm also amused and patiently awaiting Eve's answer. Will she lie or tell the truth? Or will she avoid the question entirely as she's tried to do to me since that night?

"What makes you ask that?" Eve asks.

Vicky straightens. "Dev says he only discloses his affairs on a need-to-know basis, and I don't need to know. But I think he's wrong. Secrets ruin relationships. So, I thought I'd skip the middleman and go straight to the source."

"This may sound strange since I hardly know you, but I agree with Devlin. If there's anything to know, he should be the one to deliver the news. Not all secrets are kept with bad intentions," Eve says.

"So," Vicky looks my way and raises a brow, touching her hand to my arm on the table.

Eve gives me an adorably pleading look, and I smirk. Her lips parted nervously, and I wished I had kissed them when I had the chance. If only I were the kissing kind.

"My lips are sealed," I told Vicky, still focused on Eve. Eve's mouth snaps shut, and my eyes linger on her lips.

"I appreciate this loyalty thing you two have going. Guess I can't be mad at that," Vicky says.

The server returns and sets our plates on the table. Eve breathes easier at the sight of it, and so do I. The quicker we get through lunch, the better. Vicky wasn't a bad shadow today, but her line of questioning has Eve on edge, and I don't like her discomfort at the hands of anyone but mine.

I devour my turkey on rye while Vicky does the same with her grilled cheese. Eve barely touches her salad, but her chilled glass of water is non-existent.

Vicky was surprisingly quiet on the ride back to the office and dove straight into the task I'd given her once we were inside. I assume she's thinking up new and exciting ways to rattle Eve further.

Eve disappeared inside her office without a word which is so unlike her. It's also not like me to visit her office without reason, but here I am.

I rap my knuckles on the door to gain Eve's attention, then walk inside uninvited. "We should talk." I stand in front of her desk, looking down into her eyes.

Eve clears her throat, reverting her eyes to the papers before her. "There's nothing to talk about, and if you're worried about your secret, don't. It's safe with me."

"Eve," I tried again.

"Don't get all righteous on me now, Devlin. Nothing has changed," Eve says, glancing up at me.

"Eve, Vicky is my…."

"It's none of my business. We're not friends." Eve cuts me off. "You don't owe me an explanation. Victoria is a nice girl." She smiles half-heartedly.

"She is," I agree, reflecting on when I didn't want to know Vicky.

"When did you two meet?" Eve asks, surprising me.

"I thought you didn't want to know." I stuff my hand into my pant pocket. For someone who's not my friend and not interested, Eve sure asks many questions she doesn't want the answers to.

Eve opens her mouth to speak, only to close it when Vicky walks in.

"Hey guys," Vicky says from the doorway. "Sorry to barge in again, but I need Dev's help." She waves a sheet of paper in front of her.

"Be right there," I respond, and Vicky nods, turning to leave.

I give Eve my attention once more. "We'll table this conversation until later."

"Sure," Eve says, adding under her breath as I turn and walk toward the door, "Booty calls."

I stop mid-step, smiling, despite that she just referred to my sister as a booty call, but I don't turn back around. "Did you say something, Eve?"

"I said, duty calls," she lies over the nerves in her throat.

"Duty calls," I laugh, continuing my exit.

# Chapter 9

**Evelyn**

NO ONE TABLES a conversation like me.

It's Friday, and Devlin never brought up our previous encounter. Of course, I was more than happy to pretend I didn't care. I made a fool of myself on Monday, but never again. Time has passed. My emotions are in check—have been since Victoria left the office.

I don't know what came over me. Seeing Devlin and Victoria together conjured a jealous streak I wasn't supposed to have. I shouldn't have felt Devlin belonged to me because I didn't want him.

*I don't want him.*

I submitted my proposal for the party this morning with the minimal belief that I'll win. I applied just as much enthusiasm and time as the years before, but something feels off this time. Everything about this week has been off. Why should this be any different?

I notice Devlin emerge from his office out of the corner of my eye. I remain planted, standing at the small conference table separating our offices. My heart thumps harder with every step he takes toward me.

Devlin has behaved all week, which is fine, but I miss our friendly banter. I wonder if Victoria is the cause. Did she demand that he tone it down with the ladies?

Devlin stops inches away from me, and I say the first thing that comes to mind.

"The stats on the Egg Project aren't great, but I think it's worth a shot." I lift my eyes to him, and there's absolutely nothing there to signal that he feels anything meaningful for me. Nothing.

"I agree," Devlin smiles casually, his eyes focused on mine. "But there's a more pressing matter at hand," he pauses, and I stare, wondering what could be more pressing.

"Mr. Sawyer wants to see us in the conference room," Devlin continues.

"Let me grab a pen and pad," I respond, and Devlin nods as I step away.

When I returned seconds later, I expected the room to be vacant, but Devlin was still waiting by the exit.

"Shall we?" He asks, his hand touching lightly on my back as I stroll past him.

I pretended not to notice his touch, but I felt it as if he had touched my bare skin. I stumbled over thin air as a memory of us flashed through my mind.

Devlin gently grabs my arm, keeping me upright. "Nervous?" he asks, catching my gaze.

"Not nervous," I answered, giving him a simple smile. *Just aroused.*

Susan and Jan watch us with keen eyes, whispering to each other. They're the best of friends, office gossips, and as nice as they come, but I've never fed into their hype. I didn't want my business to belong to everyone else in the office. I can only imagine what it looked like when Devlin and I left our office.

"Susan. Jan." Devlin greets, walking behind me. "Meetings about to start."

"We'll be right behind you." I recognize Jan's voice as we pass.

"Hm," Comes Susan's response after.

I grin inwardly.

Susan and Jan are not Devlin fans, unlike most women that work here. I can only imagine what he said or did to land on their bad side.

Everyone takes their usual seats in the main conference room, leaving the chair across from me bare. Charity's seat is also empty. She never misses work, much less a meeting.

The room quiets as Mr. Sawyer enters and sits at the head of the table. He clears his throat, commanding attention before he begins.

"I'm sure you've noticed, but Charity isn't in attendance today, which is why I called this meeting." Mr. Sawyer's brooding stare travels around the table.

There is no limit to the thoughts invading my mind.

*Is charity hurt, or worse, dead?*

The latter makes me sick to my stomach. I want to host the Christmas party, but not at the expense of Charity's life.

"Unfortunately, Charity fell and broke her ankle and requires surgery. Therefore, she will be out of work for a few months. She appointed Jan to take the lead until she returns. Jan, Charity will be available by phone in dire circumstances while she's recovering." Mr. Sawyer pauses, looking around the room and halting on me.

My body tenses under Mr. Sawyer's gaze. His eyes are hard, almost cold, sending a slight chill through me. He rarely gives anyone more than a two-second glance which makes me wonder. Why me?

Mr. Sawyer's eyes move away, freeing me from his grip, and I release a calming breath. He continued the meeting, asking if anyone had questions or suggestions as usual, but I barely heard the answers returned. My mind is still on Charity and Mr. Sawyer's weird behavior.

"Evelyn," Mr. Sawyer's voice breaks through my daydream minutes later.

"Yes," I answered, jumping to attention.

"Anything to add?" He questions.

"Yes. Devlin and I decided to move forward with the Egg Project. We are confident it will gain traction after a soft release with a little influence." I glance at Devlin, and he smiles, nodding his agreement.

"Excellent," Mr. Sawyer says, addressing the room again. "If there's nothing else," he pauses for a response, but everyone remains quiet. "Meeting adjourned," he says, remaining seated.

I stand to leave with everyone else, only walking a few feet when I hear my name called.

"Evelyn. I need a few minutes of your time," Mr. Sawyer says.

I turn around, and Devlin nearly crashes into me. I look up at him, and he whispers, "You were distracted, Eve."

Devlin is right. I was distracted, and his comment isn't making it any better. I guess a few days of no banter is all he can handle. Though, I'm not mad at him. I missed him.

"Not the time," I respond, side-stepping Devlin.

I've been alone with the boss before, but this time feels different, meaningful, and life-changing. Honestly, I never thought he liked me, which is confusing because he was the deciding factor in my employment.

"Have a seat," Mr. Sawyer says directly, giving me no choice but to obey.

I take Charity's seat since it's closest to the door. It provides easy access to my getaway in case he fires me. I stare at Mr. Sawyer because, as nervous as I am inside, eye contact is key.

Mr. Sawyer leans back in his chair, resting his arms on the side. It's the most relaxed I've seen him, and he's still not fully relaxed. His hard gaze seems deeper now that we're the only two in the room.

"You are the only viable candidate to host the Christmas party now that Charity is out," Mr. Sawyer begins.

My heart leaps into my throat, his words nearly choking me. I don't care if he chose me by default. It still feels good to be recognized. My proposal must have been decent, considering he didn't opt for an outside planner.

"It's a tall order, Evelyn. Potential clients will be attending. You must pull this off without a hitch," he says meaningfully. "One month. Are you sure you're up for the task?"

I was sure before he started talking. Now? I sense the doubt trying to shake my confidence.

What if I fail?

What if I lose my job over this party?

I swallow the uncertainty, straightening my back, portraying all the signs of absolution.

"I'm positive. You won't regret your decision."

"Great. As this is a company function, you're allowed time during the day to make arrangements as long as it doesn't interfere with your daily duties. You may use your company card for expenses and submit all correspondence to accounting. Any purchases outside of your proposed budget must come through me for approval. Any questions?" Mr. sawyer taps his finger on the arm of his chair impatiently.

I'm in shock. Nothing comes to mind. "Not at the moment."

"Well, I suppose congratulations are in order." Mr. Sawyer's lackluster praise doesn't deter me from my high.

"Thank you."

Mr. Sawyer dismisses me, and I stride to my office feeling like a million bucks. I finally got what I wanted. Excitement bubbles inside me, threatening a scream and shout, but I remain composed.

Devlin is in the common area and looks up when I enter. He smiles as his eyes travel the length of me. "What's the verdict? Are you staying or going?"

I suppose that depends on how well the party goes, but I can't think about that now. This victory deserves to be enjoyed and relished. I walk up to Devlin standing at the table and, without thinking, throw my arms around him.

"Whoa," Devlin says, his body stiffening. "What did I do to deserve a hug?"

I don't know. I needed to expel some of my energy before I burst, and he was the only one in the room.

I release Devlin, stepping back a fraction once I realize what I've done. "Sorry. I didn't mean…."

"No need to apologize, Eve," Devlin says, brushing his thumb over my cheek. "Your arms are always welcome." He smirks, and I blush from the embarrassment that I liked how it felt to touch him again, to have him touch me back. I'm also annoyed for the same reason. I can't believe I threw myself at him.

"My arms aren't the only ones welcome," I respond, regretting this whole encounter. "That was a mistake," I told Devlin, turning toward my office.

Devlin gently grabs my arm, halting my steps. "Eve, wait." His eyes soften, and his fingers twitch on my arm.

I stare at his hand, frowning, and he drops it.

"Why, Devlin?" I face him, crossing my arms over my chest. It's amazing how he managed to ruin my mood in less than ten seconds.

Devlin flinches like I've said something wrong. "I gather the meeting went well," he says, leaning against the table.

I fight the urge to ogle him in his suit. I've never met a man who leans quite like him. One whose eyes pull me in so fluidly. One whose voice trembles through my entire body.

"Eve," Devlin calls.

"Yes," I snap.

"The meeting."

"If you really want to know," I smile, remembering the good news.

"I do." Devlin holds my stare and a whole other thought crosses my mind at his words.

*That's not happening.*

*Not in a million years.*

I bury the thought. "You're looking at the new planner for our holiday party," I said proudly, relaxing my arms at my side.

"Congratulations. Your persistence finally paid off thanks to Charity's misfortune."

"You have such a way with words, Devlin," I reply sarcastically. He should have left it at congratulations. "Thanks anyway." I walk away before he says something else to tick me off.

# Chapter 10

*Two Weeks Later*

**Devlin**

THERE ARE FEW feelings worse than wanting something you can't have. But that yearning makes the hunt and drive to pursue that much stronger.

I never lose focus. I never lost sight of the big picture until Eve landed in my bed. Our relationship was a game of sorts. I'd flirt and say things that were sure to annoy her, and she would give me a witty comeback, pretending not to notice. We still do those things, but something has changed.

When I look at her, and she stares back, it's not just a meeting. Our eyes kiss. I lust for her.

I've never wanted to be back inside any woman as I do Eve. Fucking her was a blessing and a curse. She's all I can think about. Her thick caramel thighs, curvy hips, and plush lips that I refused to kiss have been on repeat in my mind. I can't shake, talk, or work the thoughts away.

I thought about sewing my wild oats with someone else, but it's not so appealing. A fling would only put a dent in my hunger for Eve. But maybe that's what I need to curb my appetite, even if it's only for a blip.

Eve has been focused on work and party planning for the last two weeks. She's also been avoiding the hell out of me unless work requires my input. Our offices are only a space apart, but we've talked more on the phone than in person lately.

I'm starting to feel my edge slip away. Or maybe it's taking over. Whatever the case, I need my control back.

I have a clear view of Eve from my office. She just walked back inside with a stack of papers in her hand and left the door wide open. She stops on the visitor's side of her desk, giving me a full view of her backside. It's a dress day and a fitted one at that. I know it's wrong, but I can't look away.

There are days when I think Eve does shit like this on purpose to taunt me. But that can't be the case if she's not on the market. Predictable Eve would never flaunt for any man, much less me. She knows better than to dangle beef in front of a lion. I'm liable to pounce.

I fight the urge to go to Eve until I can't fight it anymore. I'm intent on getting the reaction I've missed as I slip up behind her. The reaction she's deprived me of for weeks. I stop an inch away, and she startles, swiveling her head toward me. Her shoulder hits my chest, but I don't mind one bit.

"Stop sneaking up on me," Eve whisper-shouts.

I smile, soaking in her irritation. God, how I've missed this. "What are you working on? You look stumped."

*And smoking hot in that dress.*

My eyes fall to Eve's lips, and she looks away, refocusing on her papers.

Eve clears her throat, shifting the papers from one hand to the other, one at a time. "Christmas party," she answers.

"Well, you look…."

"Don't say distracted," Eve warns.

I chuckle, shrugging my shoulder. "I wasn't going to," I responded.

"Good because if I look *anything*, it's busy," Eve says.

She's right. She looks busy. She *is* distracting. It's hard to get anything done with her around. Her little black dress is enough to make any man want to toss his little black book.

"Anything I can help with?" I asked.

"I don't know. What do you think? Should I go with the cloth or satin tablecloth?" Eve asks, lifting the papers to eye level.

I step closer, touching my chest to her arm as I look over her shoulder. I breathe in her scent. She smells like fresh flowers, only sweeter. Her hair tickles her neck as my breath coats her skin. I place my hand on the desk and lean in for a better look, but mostly to get closer to her.

"That depends," I said.

"On what?"

"On what you plan to do with them when the party's over."

"That's not up to me. The supplies won't belong to me."

"But you could borrow them for thirty minutes to an hour. I'm sure Sawyer wouldn't mind. I do enjoy the feel of satin caressing my skin."

Eve glances my way, and I wink. She blushes, her eyes blinking rapidly as she swallows the lump in her throat.

"Devlin, this isn't a joke," Eve says nervously. "What you're implying…."

"I'm not implying anything. I'm merely stating the benefits of satin. You asked for my opinion, and I gave it."

Eve racks the papers on the desk, giving me an evil glare. "Do you take anything seriously?" She turns to face me fully, dropping the papers on the desk. "I'm not interested in your twisted opinion of satin. I don't care how it makes your skin feel. If I screw this up, my job could be on the line. So, I would appreciate it if you'd show some respect and keep your intimate thoughts to yourself. I have no interest," she claims.

Eve seems pissed, just the way I like her. Hot and bothered.

Misery loves company. I can't be the only one sulking in this tension between us. Eve may not want a relationship, but she can't deny our chemistry. I think we both realize that once is not enough, but she refuses to acknowledge it.

"Keep telling yourself that, and I'll keep pretending to believe it," I told Eve. "I'm serious about the satin, though. It presents a much more elegant feel if that's what you're aiming for. And a crystal vase would be a nice touch for the centerpiece."

Eve clears her throat, pressing her fingertips to the edge of the desk. "You do realize I'm on a budget, right?"

"I do." I lift an eyebrow.

"Well, maybe suggest something less extravagant and expensive than crystal."

I quirk my lips. "Just don't go with plastic. Sawyer would likely blow a gasket."

Eve gives me a soft smile. "That would be entertaining if I didn't mind risking my livelihood. I can feel my ass hitting the pavement just thinking about it."

Eve's eyes kiss mine again, and I want to touch her. I need to feel some part of her.

I slide my fingertips along the desk until they meet Eve's. She stiffens, allowing my touch, but only for a few seconds. Not long enough to quench my thirst, but long enough to steady my heartbeats.

Eve pulls her hand away. "I've got a lot of work to do," she explains. "Did you need something? Or are you just passing through?"

*I need more of you, Eve.*

*I want your legs spread wide, so I can claim residence and eat you like it's the last meal on earth.*

My dick twitched at the thoughts floating in my head.

"Just passing through," I answer. "But if you need help with any of this, or anything else," I offer. "I'm your number one," I remind Eve.

"I'll keep that in mind. Though, I'm sure my best friend and I can manage."

I'm not sure who her best friend is, but I'm jealous of the time they get to spend with her.

"Well, if the best friend bails, my offer stands," I said, backing toward the door. "By the way, you look nice today. And you smell divine."

Eve opens her mouth, and I turn, walking away before she responds.

I enter my office, shaking my head once inside. I can't believe I paid Eve a somewhat respectable compliment. My words usually turn naughty when I'm around her. Leaving is good. Being in her presence is making me soft.

I sit at my desk, and my cell phone rings minutes later. I stare at the screen for a moment before answering.

"Let me guess. Another favor," I said to Vicky on the other end of the line.

"Well, hello to you too," she replies. "I don't always want something when I call, Dev."

"Why else would you call me at work?"

Vicky sighs. "Because this time is different. Mom is cooking dinner on Sunday."

"And where do I fit into the equation?"

"Dad wants us to be there," Vicky answers.

The silence is eerie as I gather my thoughts.

It's not the first time I've been invited to dinner. I like Vicky's mom. She's nice. But dinner with dad is always tense. It's more like a family meeting rather than just dinner.

I should've expected it. Dad's invites, or shall I say, mandatory summons happen every quarter, and they're non-negotiable. At least, that's how I've always perceived them.

"What time is dinner?" I ask.

"Same as usual. Six o'clock sharp."

"See you then," I said.

"This totally screws my plans. But yeah, I'll see you there," Vicky says. Then she ends the call.

Vicky doesn't like family dinners any more than I do. I know her reasons for entertaining dad's wishes. But I don't understand mine. I'm a grown-ass man. I could say no. That's the thing with life, though. I've been conditioned, and now it's hard to break old habits. Besides, I wouldn't feel right leaving Vicky to fend alone.

# Chapter 11

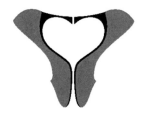

**Evelyn**

PARTY PLANNING COULDN'T have happened at a better point in my life. It's taken all my free time at the office and keeps me distracted from Devlin.

*Oh, persistent Devlin.*

Devlin wants to get beneath my fabric again for sure, and I admit, it's hard to resist him. I just can't be that woman. One time with him was not enough. It was a tease. He was a beast in bed, and I had the best sex I've had in my life, but I can't be his toy. Great sex can lead to feelings, and falling for Devlin is risky. He doesn't have a serious bone in his body. Well, not the kind that truly matters. I won't set myself up to be let down again. I don't need another John. Ending my relationship made me realize I wanted more. Being with Devlin solidified just how much more I want, how much I've missed out on.

If only I could make a man. He would be fifty percent Devlin—top-notch chemistry & great work ethic. Thirty percent John—someone kind who values home. And twenty percent mystery—someone who loves hard, who's not afraid to grow together in every way.

"There are better ways to waste a life."

My head swivels at the sound of Holland's voice. "What do you mean?" I ask, feeling slight.

Holland stares at me with an elbow resting on the folded arm across his chest. His finger and thumb tease the day-old stubble on his chin. "You've been staring at the same candle for the last two minutes. It's still a cylinder. Still brown. And the wick is sturdy as ever," he explains.

I set the candle back on the display rack and grabbed another one, turning it in my hands. "It wasn't two minutes, and these things take time," I lied, having no clue how long I was staring. Holland could've left me standing here, and I probably wouldn't have noticed.

All because of Devlin. He has invaded my mind like a dormant virus. I know he's there, but there's little I can do about him until he decides to strike. And he strikes at the worst moments. Like now. In a store as I'm shopping with Holland. The guy who never misses anything.

"I agree, but fixating on one candle for longer than one minute is a bit excessive. Don't you think?" Holland asks. "And your expressions don't lie. You're thinking about *him* again. Aren't you?"

"What do you care?" I snapped without a second thought and regretted it immediately.

I set the candle down and faced Holland, joining our hands.

"I'm sorry. I didn't mean it. I… Ugh! He makes me crazy," I admit.

"You were crazy before you banged him," Holland surmised, flashing a crooked smile.

I slap his arm. "Not accurate," I said.

Holland raises an eyebrow. "I'm gonna say something that you won't like," he warns.

I tilt my head. "Please don't tell me I'm in love with the devil because that is far from the truth."

I notice an older woman passing us, smiling cautiously with a confused look on her face, and I smile back at her. She probably thinks I'm insane if she was listening in.

Holland glanced her way, returning her smile, then looked at me. "Not in love," he continues after the woman is out of earshot. "But there is something there worth exploring. You wouldn't be this uptight if there weren't."

I give Holland an incredulous stare. "Are you encouraging my slutty behavior?" I ask. "You're supposed to talk me down from the ledge, not spur me to jump."

"All I'm saying is, there may be more to it than just lust. Devlin may want more from you than he's letting on. And some part of you feels the same."

I guffawed. "Please. Devlin is not that type of guy. We've discussed this. Remember? He's hit and quit." I pause, remembering how close we were when I saw him last. His warm minty breath and solid chest. His fingertips brushing mine. "I must be loco," I said, shaking my head. "I can't shake him. Something about him is so enticing, but he's bad for my sanity. If I allow him any closer than he has already gotten, he'll likely break me. And that's saying something because I'm as tough as they come."

"I think you're afraid to let anyone in," Holland says.

"How can you say that? I let you in, and you're still here."

"That's different. We're different. Take you and John, for instance. You were together for years, and you only allowed him to scratch the surface of who you are," Holland says. "I know you better than he did, and you lived with the guy."

I turn away from Holland, picking up and examining another candle. "I'm not afraid. I let people in. Devlin just can't be one of those people."

Holland and my eyes move to a young woman who stops next to us. "Can I help you find anything?" She asks. Her mouth and eyes greet Holland before glancing at me. She's not the type that Holland would usually go for—medium height, fair skin, frizzy ponytail, a button nose, no makeup, and a sweet voice. She reminds me of myself, only a few years younger.

"We've got it covered. My girl here is a snail when it comes to decision-making. But thanks," Holland responded.

"Well, if you need anything, let me know," the woman says, dripping her eyes over Holland.

My cheese turns to a full grin when she walks away. Holland's forehead wrinkles, his eyes following her until she disappears.

"Who's afraid now?" I ask Holland.

Holland is not shy when it comes to women, but he does tend to push the right kind of woman away. I guess Holland and I are alike in a way. I'm the only woman he's allowed to know him, and he's that person for me. We haven't been emotionally available to anyone but each other. Maybe that's the problem.

"What?" Holland feigns innocence.

"*You* know what. That woman was flirting with you, and you shrugged it off like it was nothing."

"She was doing her job."

I bring the candle to my face, wrinkling my nose at the scent, then set it back down. "She was, but she's also into you. You're oblivious," I told him.

"I know when a woman is flirting with me. That was not it," Holland says.

"You know when a demoralized woman is flirting. Like I said, oblivious."

"You're delusional."

"Maybe, but I'm right."

"How did the conversation get focused on me?" Holland asks.

I flash a smile. "You know what we should do?"

"You have that crazy look in your eyes you'd get when we were teens."

I wiggle my brow. "We should go on a date." It's not the most absurd idea I've ever had. Devlin was, and I need to get over him.

"Already told you. *We* are not a good idea." Holland crossed his arms over his chest.

"Not me and you," I grin. "With other people. I'll choose someone for you," I said, nodding to the woman that walked away. "And you choose for me. Anyone but Devlin," I clarify.

Holland looks skeptical, unwilling to humor me, but he rarely tells me no.

"Come on. If nothing else, we'll get a good laugh out of it," I pressed my palms together, trying to convince Holland.

"What the hell? It can't hurt," Holland relents.

I picked up the second candle I had held since we were here and forced it into Holland's hand. "Good. I've decided on this one. Stay here."

"Where are you going?" Holland voices as I walk away.

"To fulfill a woman's wish." I wink at Holland, then disappear.

# Chapter 12

**Devlin**

IF ONLY CONTINUING through the circular driveway and leaving was an acceptable option.

I stare at my dad's overcompensated home once outside my car. It's much too big for just him and his wife, Shana. Though, I guess the same could be said about my home. I don't get what she sees in him or why she stayed all these years. They never smile at each other or show any signs of affection. The only explanation I could come up with is that he threatened her with Vicky. Honestly, I wouldn't put it past him after learning of his and my mother's relationship. The only difference between Vicky and me is that he wanted her. I'm just a casualty of unfortunate events that my mother refused to let him forget.

I sigh heavily outside the front door, then ring the bell. Thankfully, Vicky is the first face I see.

"Good. You're here," Vicky says, pulling me inside.

The air is comfortable and warm, but the atmosphere is as cold as ice, making it hard to breathe evenly. I always feel like I lose a piece of myself in this house, like life is being sucked out of me. The only way to get it back is to get through dinner and leave.

"Where else would I be?" I chuckle at the only bright side to all of this. If it weren't for Vicky, I would risk being shunned by the family.

"I don't know," Vicky shrugs. "Working overtime with that hot partner...."

"Vicky," I warn. "Now is not the time."

"I know. I know. But I need to do something to get my mind off of this foolery." She wraps her arm around mine.

"Where's Dad and Shana?"

"Dad's still upstairs getting ready as if he's attending a business party." Vicky rolls her eyes. "Mom's setting the table," she adds, wrinkling her nose. "You can call her mom, you know."

I lift a brow. That will never happen in a million years, and Vicky knows it. It's not the first time she's suggested it to get under my skin, though. Shana is only ten years older than I am. It would be too weird. She was a child when I was born. Still a minor when I turned seven. Dad always had a thing for younger women. I guess Shana is his midlife crisis.

"I have a mother," I responded with a hint of irritation. My mother may not be present, but that doesn't change who she was.

Vicky giggles. "Easy, Dev. No need to spark a fire."

"Let's get this over with," I told her.

"As you wish," she says, leading me toward the dining room.

The three of us sit awkwardly at the table, with Vicky and me sitting opposite each other. Two chairs are on either side of us, separating us from the heads of the table—one end where Shana sits and the other where my dad will soon occupy.

Shana outdid herself as usual. Dinner looks and smells delicious. Steam rises from the plates in front of us, coupled with glasses of water and wine, but no one dares to take a bite yet.

Vicky wrinkles her nose at the glass of sparkling cider in front of her, drawing a smile from me. Dad doesn't condone underage drinking, especially when it comes to his princess, Victoria. But I have a feeling her palate has already been tainted. He just doesn't know it, or he refuses to believe it.

"So, Devlin," Shana says, smiling. "Still no plus one, I see."

Even if I had a plus one, dad likely wouldn't allow it unless we were hitched. He's such a hypocrite, wanting to dictate his children's lives as if they were his. He never allowed us to make mistakes, but I've made plenty behind his back.

I smile back at Shana. "Not for the foreseeable future."

"I told you, mom. Dev's a lifer. He refuses to let anyone break that tough shell of his. He's going to end up wrinkled and alone in his castle," Vicky says teasingly.

Vicky just may be right. I have no desire to wife anyone. Though, there is one woman I wouldn't mind fucking continuously.

"There has to be someone that caught your eye," Shana says.

Vicky kicks my foot under the table, clearing her throat, and I give her a warning glare.

At that moment, dad strides in, suit-clad, broad chest and hard-lined jaw. He greets Shana with a temple kiss, then sits at the head of the table. His presence commands everyone's attention.

Dad spreads a cloth napkin over his lap and releases a slow breath, his eyes moving from Vicky to me. "I'm glad you both could make it," he says as if he expected anything less.

"If I may ask," I said to dad. "Why the urgent invite?"

Dad clears his throat. "We'll get to that. But first, let's eat," he says, his eyes flitting to Shana, who beams a smile at him.

*Not weird at all.*

I sip my water before diving into my meal.

I lean back in my chair when I'm done, rubbing my hand over my belly. "Thanks, Shana. Dad. I needed that," I told them. If for no other reason, a full stomach made being here worth it.

Shana nods her acceptance.

"Glad you enjoyed it," Dad says. "It may be your last home-cooked meal for a while. Well, at least from Shana."

"What do you mean?" Vicky asks with a mix of curiosity and appreciation.

Dad looks at Shana. "Would you like to tell them? Or should I?" he asks.

Whatever *it* is, Dad doesn't seem ecstatic about it. Then again, not much excites him.

"Come on, Mom. Don't keep us in suspense," Vicky says.

Shana takes a deep breath, her smile brighter now. "Well, your father and I are having a baby."

Vicky's mouth drops open, the smile dropping from her face. "What?" She asks incredulously.

A shocked chuckle leaves me. Then I raise the wine glass to my mouth and take a few sips. Never in a million years would I have guessed this news. Never. Vicky was supposed to be their only child last I was informed. I wonder what changed. Did they come to this decision together? Or did karma decide to throw dad a curveball?

Dad looks as if he doesn't quite believe the words himself.

"You're going to be a big sister," Shana rephrased, focusing on Vicky. "And you, a big brother again," she says to me.

"I don't know what to say." Vicky furrows her brows.

*Me either.*

I rub my palm over my mouth, letting the message sink in. "I guess congratulations are in order," I said to Shana.

"How far along are you?" Vicky asks, picking up the apple cider she loves to hate and sipping.

Shana's smile falters for a moment as she cuts her eyes at dad. "Further than we imagined. Four months. Which is why we called you here. We wanted you to be the first to know."

Vicky sets her glass down and looks at dad. "But you…" She pauses, moving her eyes to Shana. "And you're…." She stops again. "I mean, I'm happy if you're happy. I'm sorry. It's just hard to wrap my head around."

Dad's nose flares, but he remains quiet, calming himself before speaking. "I know it's not ideal, unplanned," he says. "But it's happening, and there's nothing we can do about it. Shana is happy, and that's all that matters."

An awkward, wordless exchange passes between dad and Shana.

What I wouldn't give to have been a fly on the wall when dad found out.

"What about you?" Vicky asks Dad.

Dad looks at Vicky. "Whatever your mother wants," he responded.

Dad's answer, tone, and posture say everything. He doesn't want another child, but Shana does. For once, I'm glad to be here. It was worth it to see the look on dad's face. I only wish Shana wasn't the recipient of his cruelty.

"I need some fresh air," I blurted. "Vicky, why don't you join me," I said, sensing she could use the break too.

I grab my wine glass and stand. Then, Vicky and I leave the table without objection.

Standing on the front porch, I drink my wine, leaving a few sips in the glass.

"Here," I offer Vicky, and she takes it, gulping the last drops without flinching.

*So, my inkling was right.*

"Thanks," Vicky says, returning the glass to me.

"It's not the worst thing to happen," I told her.

"And the bright side is?" She asks.

"Dad's focus isn't solely on you anymore."

Vicky sighs. "True, but they're old."

I chuckle. "Your mom is not old. Dad is. Besides, she's happy, and that's what matters."

"I guess you're right. It wouldn't be the worst thing to have a younger sibling to dote on," Vicky says.

"Especially if *he* grew up to be like me," I added.

"Maybe. Just less afraid of commitment." Vicky bumps my side with her shoulder.

"There's nothing wrong with being alone," I counter.

"I agree, but it is a problem when you're presented with a chance not to be, and you refuse to try," she points out.

I know she's thinking of Eve. But why should I risk opening my heart to someone who isn't ready? I'm not the guy who gets his heart broken. I'm the guy who breaks hearts. The guy who leaves them wanting more. Everyone except Eve, apparently. She sticks out that she wants nothing more from me. She left *me* wanting more. I hate this foreign feeling and love it all the same.

*What the fuck has Eve done to me?*

My forehead wrinkles as I stare into the night.

"Dev, you okay?" Vicky asks.

"Yeah. I'm fine. Are you good to go back inside?"

"Yep. And about that drink. Some would say it's better to ease into it with family than dive in with friends. You won't mention it to Dad, will you?" Vicky asks.

I grin. "My lips are sealed this time."

# Chapter 13

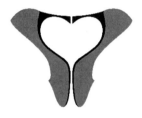

*One Week Later*

**Evelyn**

WAS I DRINKING?

Second-guessing myself, I sit at the bar in Lynah's restaurant for my blind date to show up.

I can't believe I let Holland choose my date. I'm too young to be in crisis, but I must've been because here I am, following through with one of my most questionable choices. I can think of better ways to spend Friday night after the work week I've had.

"Can I get you a drink?" The bartender asks for the second time in ten minutes.

I offer a smile. "I'll give him five more minutes," I said of my late date.

I arrived three minutes early, not wanting to appear too eager, but not late either. I guess Lenox likes to make an entrance.

"Five minutes and, I'm sorry, but you'll have to place an order or free the bar," the bartender warns.

"Thank you." Five minutes is all I need. At this point, I'm hoping Lenox doesn't show. Then I wouldn't have to go through with this farce.

One minute later, I see a guy approaching through the bar mirror, and I pray to God it's not him. But he's looking right at me. And smiling at me. He stops right next to me, and I close my eyes for a second, rolling them inwardly.

"Holland told no lies," he says, his eyes roaming over me. "You must be, Evelyn."

My eyes meet his, and I wish I had worn pants instead of a dress. My skin crawls, warning me to flee. He doesn't look half bad, but he's giving off creepy vibes.

"I am. And your name?" I ask to be sure I have the right creep.

"Lenox Bates." He sucks his bottom lip into his mouth and releases it. "It's a pleasure to meet you."

*The pleasure is not mine.*

Holland has some explaining to do. I was fair to him. He wasn't turned off by his date. Skeptical, maybe, but not turned off. Where did he find this guy?

I plaster a smile, unable to voice a response.

"Shall we?" Lenox asks, and I stand.

I move away from the bar with Lenox at my side as we approach the Host.

"Table for Bates," Lenox says to the Host.

"Right this way," She replied.

Lynah's is dimly lit at this time of evening. It's a setting meant for lovers, but that's far from what Lenox and I are. I can't fathom why I agreed to let him pick the place—another of my questionable choices. If it were up to me, we'd be eating bagels for dinner at a well-lit and familiar cafe.

I'm seated across from Lenox at a wall booth with leather seats that extend past the top of our heads. I hadn't thought this through at all. With no pre-planned topics to discuss, I'm smiling at Lenox, and he's gazing at me.

Our drink order is taken, and I refuse anything but water with lemon. I won't have another Devlin situation on my hands.

"So, Evelyn, Holland told me you're a Brand Manager and a workaholic," Lenox breaks the silence.

I wonder what else Holland told him.

"Just passionate about my job," I replied. "And you. How do you spend your days?" I ask.

"Sweating with women," Lenox shrugs. "And men."

My eyes widen as I prepare to run.

Lenox's raised hand and chuckle stop me. "I'm a personal trainer," he explains. "You should stop by the gym sometime. I would love to work on you."

"Hm," I mumbled. *Well damn.* I clear my throat, replaying Lenox's words in my head. I'm not the smallest egg in the carton, but that's not a bad thing. I can't decide if Lenox is flirting or insulting me. Either way, it doesn't matter because, after tonight, I'll never see him again.

The waiter brings our drinks and takes our food order. Lenox orders a salad with salmon. I request Salisbury Steak with extra gravy and mashed potatoes on purpose, hoping it will turn him off.

I learn a few things about Lenox during dinner. He chews with his mouth open. He has more pictures of his dog than his family. He runs three miles every morning. He's four years younger than me, which wouldn't be so bad if he were more mature. And he loves his job too, just not for all the right reasons.

"Wanna dance?" Lenox asks after we're done eating.

I was thinking more on the lines of dessert, but I guess that's out. It's fine, though. The quicker we're done, the quicker I can leave.

I smile, thinking of an excuse. "The dance floor is nearly empty," I responded, looking around.

Mellow tunes play in the background. Two couples occupy the small dance floor in the back. Maybe I'd be into it if the music weren't so slow.

"Come on. It'll be fun," Lenox tried again. He stands, offering his hand before I can object again.

*Well, this is awkward.*

I look around the room, noticing a few eyes on us, and decide not to embarrass Lenox. "One dance. Then, I have to go," I said, placing my hand in his.

Smiles of approval lead us to the dance floor.

Lenox pulls me close, resting his hands on my waist. I put my hands on his shoulders as we sway to the music.

"See, this isn't so bad now. Is it?" Lenox asks.

"No." It's actually not bad. I only wish he were someone else.

John and I never danced like this. We rarely went out on dates after moving in together. He was the opposite of Lenox. Maybe that's why Holland chose this guy. Because, like Devlin, Lenox isn't looking for anything serious, either.

The song ends, and instead of pulling away, as another tune begins to play, I wrap my arms around Lenox's neck and lay my head on his chest, imagining it's Devlin's heart beating in my ear. Devlin's arms wrapped around me further. Devlin's palm inching over the curve of my ass.

*My ass.*

My head snaps up as I realize what's happening.

117

"Wait. No," I protested quietly, dropping my hands between Lenox and me. "What are you doing?"

Lenox has the nerve to look confused. "I thought you were into it," he explains, maintaining his hold on me.

"Well, I'm not. Let me go," I said through gritted teeth, fists pushing at his chest.

"Let's not make a scene, Evelyn," Lenox says, his voice laced with kind malice.

"Let's not," A distinct voice said behind me.

*Devlin.*

*Devlin?*

"The lady said she's not into it," Devlin continues, stepping to our side. "I suggest you listen," he said smoothly.

"Who the hell are you?" Lenox seethes.

Devlin smirks, unphased, cool, and collected. "I'm the guy you don't want to cross," Devlin answers. "If you ever want to touch another woman again, I advise you to take your fucking hands off her." His fiery eyes warn Lenox against testing him.

Lenox drops his hands, flaring his nostrils as he backs up a fraction.

"Good choice," Devlin says to Lenox. Then, he looks at me and grabs my hand. "I'm taking you home," he says, leaving no room for dispute.

I nod, remaining quiet, wondering where he came from. Was he following me? I'll have to ask him later. Right now, I'm just glad he appeared.

"I'm not paying for your half," Lenox fumes.

"No worries. Her dinner is on me," Devlin says.

I swallow, my panties damp from Devlin's behavior, his presence. I should be pissed with both of them, but I can't be mad at Devlin regardless of how hard I try. As we walk away with his hand light on my back, I allow myself to be his damsel. Eyes that, once approved, follow us.

Devlin drops a Grant on the table as we pass and ushers me outside. He pressed my back to the building a few feet from the entrance, eyes hard and unforgiving, one hand holding my arm and the other flattened against the stone wall next to my head.

Our roles are reversed. Devlin appears angry enough to punch a hole through the wall, and I'm in the mood to mix chemicals. Adrenaline floods my veins, and I tilt my chin, hoping tonight's the night he breaks his stupid rule and kisses me.

"What the hell were you thinking, Eve?" Devlin's words slapped me, bringing me back to reality.

"Me? What are you thinking?" I asked, pushing at his rugged chest. "I'm on a date."

"Who is that dipshit? Do you even know him?" Devlin asks.

"No. It's a blind date, hence the whole getting to know someone scene. What are you doing here anyway? Were you following me?"

Devlin drops his arm from the building, his fingers pinching my chin. "I was having dinner when I saw you on the dancefloor," he explained. "You should count yourself lucky. I saved you from embarrassment and possibly something worse," he says.

I push at his chest again. "I don't need the Devil to save me," I fire back. "I had it under control."

"Did you now?" Devlin asks.

"Always do," I answered.

"From where I sat, you seemed *out* of control. It appeared you were enjoying it."

"Then, why did you interrupt?" I challenge.

"Because," Devlin paused, narrowing his eyes. "I'm your number one, or did you forget?" he asks, brushing his thumb over my lips.

I knock his hand away from my mouth, discarding the words that I know to be true. "I don't belong to you, Devlin. I can date whomever I want. Dance with who I want. I can enjoy someone else's touch." *Even if it's you I'm thinking of when they touch me.* "And *if* I want more, it's my choice. I don't need *you*," I said, punching his chest with my finger.

"You're right. You don't need me. Just like I don't need you. But *want* is a damn near compelling force, Eve," Devlin says, caressing my cheek with his fingers. He glances at my lips, his finger traveling my neck and stopping just above my cleavage. "You can try and fight it, but the itch won't go away until it's scratched," he smirks. "Maybe not even then," he winks.

My panties are soaked, and my temper flares because everything he said is true. I wanted him. I still want him. We scratched the itch, and it only made things worse. The itch has become a painful annoyance, spreading through me like wildfire.

"You're impossible."

"I'm *the* possible," Devlin says.

"Screw you, Devlin."

"I'm willing whenever you're ready. Now, how about that ride home?"

"I drove. So, thanks. But no thanks," I said, storming off toward my car.

Who does Devlin think he is, coming to my rescue and making me feel things I don't want to feel?

# Chapter 14

**Devlin**

EVE IS MAKING me crazy.

As I watch her in her office, Friday night's events replay in my head.

Though she didn't know, I did drive by her house that night to ensure she arrived home safely. Seeing her with that asshole messed with my head. He didn't have the right to touch her as he had. I had to be sure he didn't follow her. I'm a hypocrite, but my intentions are good.

I don't understand why she would go on a blind date when she could've been with me. My ego may have been bruised a bit. I was furious that she'd put herself at risk. How could she be so careless?

And to think, I almost stayed in that night. Who knows what could've happened?

I shake my head, looking at the open file on my desk. Eve and I are scouring for the next big thing now that the Egg Project is in full production, but it's been hard to focus.

I swear she's taunting me, changing me somehow.

I was on a date of my own Friday night, my first in months. India, a woman I'd just met at the bar, had taken a bathroom break just as I noticed Eve. I couldn't fight the urge to go to her. I intended to say hello, just to rattle her, then return to my table. But when I heard her say *no*, it triggered something else inside me. Something primal, protective.

It's not like me to skip out before the evening is over. While we had just met, India was not happy when I returned. She'd witnessed me escorting Eve outside and thought I had bailed on her, which was a viable option if Eve hadn't driven her car.

There Eve was, escaping her date, acknowledging he was a creep because he wanted her to put out. While my date thought I was a creep because I refused what she offered.

I could've accepted India's request to follow her home after dinner, but not that night. Not with thoughts of Eve on my mind. Instead, I went home alone, had a drink, and pumped my cock for an embarrassingly short amount of time to visions of Eve until I erupted on the shower wall.

My desk phone rings, revealing Sawyer's name.

"Hughes, speaking," I answered.

"Join me in the conference room in ten," Sawyer says.

"Should I notify Evelyn?" I ask.

"No. It concerns other matters," he says cryptically.

"See you then," I said.

Sawyer ends the call without another word.

I gather my pen and notepad minutes later, glancing at Eve on the way out. Her eyes are still lowered, concentrating on her task. She's been that way all morning. Aside from a swift hello, I haven't heard a peep from her. Maybe I went too far this time.

"Jan," I nod, and she wrinkles her nose at me in the hallway as we pass each other, putting a smile on my face. She doesn't like me very much, and I can't fathom why. I've never spoken to her about anything but work. I always smile. I'm always kind, never flirted. Yet, she frowns when she looks at me.

I'm thrown aback when I enter the conference room. The head Executives surround the table with Sawyer at the head, which usually signals something important, especially if I'm invited. I'm only invited to these things when certain things need to be voted on. I close the door behind me, pausing where I stand.

"Have a seat, Devlin, "Sawyer says, motioning to my usual chair.

I sit, catching the eyes of everyone at the table before landing on Sawyer.

"I've called this meeting today to announce that I'll be scaling back my hours in preparation for retirement in a few years," Sawyer begins. "You may have noticed, but I'm not as young as I used to be," he deadpans.

The urge to laugh is strong as I glance around the table at everyone's faces. They're too serious for my liking. Normally, I wouldn't speak until asked, but I'm in a *fuck it* kind of mood.

"I think we can all agree on that," I respond, chuckling.

Throats clear. Eyes widen. A few even smile.

My eyes cautiously return to Sawyer, and I catch a faint glimpse of a smile before he clears his throat.

"There will be changes ahead, starting with one key element," Sawyer continued. "You all know Devlin Hughes," he says, nodding to me. "Devlin has proven himself a worthy pupil, working his way up from the bottom since he was first employed. He knows the semantics of each department. He's well educated and possesses the knowledge and experience needed to advance to the next level."

I knew this day was coming. I just didn't know it would be this soon. I don't know if I'm ready for the next level, but I smile confidently, pretending to be. It's a once-in-a-lifetime opportunity. It's what I've worked so hard for all my life. It was the intention when Sawyer hired me and why I was warned to refrain from fraternizing with my co-workers.

There is one downside. Advancing to the next level would make me Eve's superior. It makes her off-limits to me. It may even make us enemies, given that she thinks she has a shot at the position.

"In the coming months, Devlin will work closely with me to learn the ins and outs of what I do. What this means for you is that, eventually, Devlin will conduct meetings. Any correspondence, issues, and plans will go through him. He will be the Executive in charge of all operations," Sawyer says.

Regardless of the downside, my chest swells a little at my accomplishment. I'm the youngest in the room. I've been granted an opportunity that most will never have because I deserve it—because Sawyer trusts me above everyone else.

"More information will follow as we progress, but in the meantime, be patient with us as we transition. Devlin, if there's someone here that you're not familiar with, please introduce yourself once the meeting adjourns." Sawyer focused his hard eyes on me.

I'm shocked he knows the word, please. Old age must agree with him. "Will do," I said.

"Are there any questions?" Sawyer addresses the room.

I look around the room again, noticing the concern on a few faces, but everyone remains quiet, knowing nothing they say will change the outcome.

The meeting adjourns seconds later. I catch sight of Eve as I exit the conference room. She stops walking when she notices me, clutching the coffee cup in her hand. I give her a half smile that she doesn't return. Our eyes lock across the space, and I take a few steps toward her.

"Devlin," Sawyer's voice sounds behind me.

I pause, turning slightly to look back. "Yes," I answered.

"My office," he says.

I nod, turning back to Eve. She remains for a moment, staring at me with a blank look on her face. When I take the next step, she turns away, walking toward our office. I want to follow her, but I'm torn. I don't like the distance between us; from this point, I fear it will only worsen. The flirting, the bickering, my need to protect her has to stop.

"Devlin," Sawyer calls again.

"Coming," I said, moving in the opposite direction of Eve.

MY MEETING WITH Sawyer turned out to be a warning.

Sawyer noticed how I looked at Eve and advised me to shut it down before someone got hurt. Or worse, we're hit with a lawsuit. He warned me when I began working here that any relationship that wasn't platonic could not last. Unless I did a silly thing like get married, and that's not happening.

Two knocks on my office door draw my attention. I look up to Eve standing in the doorway.

"Mind if I come in?" She asks.

"Not at all," I respond, trying to be professional.

Being around her and not saying what I want to say, not acting the way I want to, and not allowing my eyes to view her the way she should be will be hard. It *is* hard. And the closer she gets to me, the harder the bulge grows in my slacks.

*Fuck, Eve. What have you done to me?*

*What have I done?*

Eve stops in front of my desk. "What was that about earlier? Your meeting with the Execs?" She asks.

I ponder how much I should tell her. If I should say anything or wait for her to hear it from Sawyer. The thought of backing away from her in any capacity withers my hardened cock.

I stand, walk around the desk, and sit on the edge facing her.

"It hasn't been announced yet, but I'm being promoted," I told Eve.

Eve's eyes pop. Then her forehead wrinkles as if she's thinking about something. "That's... that's great," she says unconvincingly.

I grip the edge of the desk on either side of me to keep from touching her. "Yeah. Sawyer is planning for retirement and appointed me his pupil. It'll be six or seven months, give or take, before the official switch, but yeah."

"So, that means I'll have to vibe with someone else soon, huh?" Eve smiles sadly.

"Maybe," I shrug. "Maybe not. You're capable of managing on your own. I don't see a reason to hire a replacement for me. Do you?"

If I have anything to say about it, there will be no replacement unless Eve desires one. And even then, it would have to be a woman. No other man will take my place here.

"Uhm. I guess not. I was practically running things with you here anyway," Eve jokes.

I laugh. "You know this means I'll be your boss, right?"

"Yes, but let's not jump ahead of ourselves. Minds can change," Eve says, dropping her eyes to my lips for a second. She clears her throat, her eyes returning to mine.

"Eve," I pause, gazing into her eyes. "I wanted to apologize for Friday night. I only wanted to help. If I offended you, I'm sorry."

"Apology accepted."

"My date will never forgive you for ruining our night, though."

"Wait. You were on a date?" Eve asks, backing up a fraction.

This is going to be harder than I thought. I don't know when to stop talking or when to say the right thing. How am I supposed to be Eve's boss?

"I was."

"And you offered to drive me home?" Eve questions.

"I did."

"So, you would've left her there?"

"I would have. For you," I admit honestly.

Eve shakes her head. "And here I was, thinking you were a knight, that you had grown some decency. You're an even bigger ass than I thought."

"Eve."

"Don't, Devlin," she whisper-shouts, a disapproving grin following. "You know what. This promotion of yours may be the best thing to come between us. I wish you all the best," she says, giving me her back and walking away.

I want to stop her, but I don't. She's right. It's for the best. Distance is good. And what better way to keep that distance than to have her hate me even more?

# Chapter 15

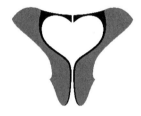

*One Week Later*

**Evelyn**

I TAPPED MY FEET against the pristine beige and white marble floor, marveling at my vision brought to life before me. Tables drenched in red and white satin. A thin vase at the center of each one houses a single white lily. Okay. So, it's not the traditional Christmas décor, but I adore lilies.

Taking a few steps, I run my fingers along the soft material as I stroll. I reposition a piece of china that seems out of place. Then I let out a comforting sigh.

I'm a bit of a perfectionist, I guess. One dish, glass, or anything that isn't positioned right is disastrous to me, especially with what was at stake.

I wasn't happy that Charity broke her ankle, not at all. But it couldn't have come at a better time. I was excited for the chance to prove myself, and I pray for a speedy recovery for Charity—after the Christmas Party is over.

I'm just glad the day is finally here.

I've kept my distance from Devlin, and he's made no advances toward me. He's been spending a lot of time with Mr. Sawyer while I finished up last-minute touches for tonight. The break has been nice but also lonely. I hate to think it, but I will miss him when he transfers to his new position.

I guess I should consider myself lucky I didn't fall for him. It's the attraction I'm struggling to wean myself of the most.

"You're doing it again," Holland accused, stopped by my side.

"Doing what?" I asked.

"Admiring my work of art," he claimed.

"Your work? Really Holly?" I teased, knowing he hated that name.

"You know I hate it when you call me that," he says earnestly.

"I know, and that's exactly why I did it," I responded snidely.

"It's a girl's name, Eve. I thought we were friends," he

134

says, bumping his shoulder against mine.

"It is, and we are," I fired back. "Hey," I said, turning to face Holland fully. "Do you remember when that guy was flirting with me at the club when we were younger, and I mentioned that I was waiting for my friend Holly who was in the bathroom?"

"Yeah. And? What does that have to do with this conversation?" Holland asks.

"The look on that guy's face when you came back and I introduced you was priceless." I shrugged. "Just saying. The name comes in handy. He was expecting a girl and got a broad chest instead," I explained, giggling. "You may have saved my life that night, Holly," I teased again.

Holland huffs out a frustrated breath, knowing that I'm right. "True, but I still don't like the name. You're lucky you're so cute," he says pointedly. He glances over my shoulder. "The place does look nice, though. You've outdone yourself," he compliments, tapping his finger against his chin and effectively changing the subject.

"You think so?" I asked.

He shrugs. "I don't see the big deal about hosting this party, but yeah. You deserve whatever accolades come from this."

Holland furrows his brow at something behind me, then grabs my shoulders.

"Don't look now, but your guy just walked in."

"My guy? I don't have a…." My words trail off as realization dawns on me. "Devlin." His name slipped from my mouth as my blood began to simmer. I try turning to confirm my suspicions, but Holland holds me firmly in place.

"I said, don't look. Unless you want him to think we were talking about him."

"Fine," I said. "But what is he doing here so early? And where is everyone else?" I wondered aloud, trying to keep my attention away from Devlin.

"Good question," Holland says. "They should be arriving by now." He let go of my arms and pulled out his phone. "It's less than an hour until showtime."

I turn toward the door, and my eyes lock on Devlin. I suck in a breath at the sight of him. I foolishly allow my eyes to roam over his body as he stalks toward me. He looks good enough to eat in his all-black attire, but I know better than to go there, even though my body betrays me.

Devlin's lips curve into a smile as he stops inches away from me. He lifts the tail of his jacket and tucks his hand into his pants pocket.

I can't speak, and he knows it by the look in his eyes.

"Eve." My name slithers from Devlin's mouth to my ears, just like the snake he is. "You clean up nicely," he says, his eyes sliding across my skin.

*So do you.*

I push the thought back as soon as it appears.

Holland clears his throat next to me. "I don't think we've met. Holland," he says, holding out his hand to Devlin, who stares at it for a moment before shaking it.

"Devlin." He gives Holland a wary, almost challenging look before returning his attention to me. His brow rose slightly. "You're plus one?" He asks.

"Yes, but..." The sudden feel of Holland's arm on my back halts my words. I look up at him, wondering why he did it, and he gives me a tight smile in return. I look back at Devlin. "Yes," I said again without the impending explanation.

Why should I care what he thinks of my relationship status? He's not interested in me. His interest is in toying with me, nothing more. And he made sure that I knew it the day I slipped up. He's made sure of it every day since.

It was a mistake climbing into Devlin's bed that night months ago. I didn't mean for it to happen, but a bad breakup and alcohol do not mix well with Devlin. He took advantage of my grief, and I let him. He's always known how to get under my skin. Hence, the reason I started dating someone else in the first place—to keep my mind off of him.

"And you? Who's the unlucky lady tonight?" I asked, staring straight into his eyes.

"I had someone in mind, but apparently, she's taken," Devlin says, matching my stare. "The night's still young,

137

though. Anything can happen," he says smugly.

Holland pulls me closer to him, catching my attention. "Eve, we should probably go check on the delay."

"Yeah. Yes, you're right. Devlin, enjoy the party. We have some things to attend to," I said. My shoulder brushes across his arm as I step around him and head for the exit.

"What was that?" Holland asked once we were outside.

"What was what?" I feign innocence.

"That thing between you two. I thought you said he didn't want you."

"He doesn't, and even if he did, I don't want him," I lied.

Holland gives me a—*I don't believe you for one second*—stare.

"What, Holly?" I said to piss him off. "It was one night that I'll never repeat. Devlin is nothing but trouble, and everything he touches turns to ruin. Besides, he's going to be my boss. Rules win."

Two cars roll into the parking lot. I recognize them as employees right away; Jan and Susan from the Design Team. Some of my tension eases away at their presence. Jan does not look happy as the two walk toward us.

"Hey," Susan greets." For a moment, I didn't think we'd make it in time."

"The important thing is you did," I smile and lean in to hug them. It's not normal behavior for us, but it's the Holidays, and I'm in a good mood.

"Yeah," Jan says. "By the way, have you seen Devlin?"

Susan twists her mouth in disgust.

"He's inside," I answered.

"He nearly killed us on the highway. When I saw him driving like a bat out of hell, weaving through traffic, I knew something would go wrong. As it turns out, seconds before he skirted past us, he'd run a red light and effectively caused a pileup. A word of advice," Jan continues. "Stay far away from him. He's trouble," she says, nearly out of breath.

If Jan only knew how hard I'm trying to stay away. I'm surprised she's holding a conversation with me. I suppose she has the holiday bug too.

"When I looked in my rearview after hearing a loud crash and saw him coming, I panicked," Jan continued. "If it weren't for those tiny lines on the road's side causing a ruckus beneath my tire, I would've hit the side rail. Instead, I hit my brakes and pulled over to catch my breath, and the jerk drove right past us as if nothing happened."

*So, he's the reason everyone is late.*

"Wow," is all I could say to that. Devlin never ceases to amaze me, but rarely in a good way.

"Tell me about it. It took some time before my nerves returned to normal," Jan says. "The accident was starting to clear up when I left."

Guests and vendors began to file in shortly after Jan and Susan arrived. Holiday music in the background kept everyone's attention, and thankfully so, because there was still one thing missing—dinner.

"They'll be here," Holland tries to reassure me.

I glanced at the time on my phone again, and just before panic set in, the truck drove into the parking lot.

"See, I told you. Nothing to worry about," Holland says, rubbing my arms soothingly.

Everything had fallen into place. Holland ventured away to mingle with the guests while I ushered the catering crew inside through the back entrance, leaving them to set up.

I step through the door, stopping in my tracks. Devlin is there, waiting outside the kitchen, leaning against the wall, oozing appeal. My eyes latch onto his, desire coiling through me.

I shake my head, wrenching my eyes away, refusing to let him pull me in further.

My feet move, intent on skirting past. "Devlin," I said, staring straight ahead. I try my best to ignore him, but he refuses to allow it. He grabs my arm and pulls me against his chest, stealing my breath.

*Not now, Devlin.*

*Not tonight.*

*Not ever.*

"What are you doing?" My eyes shoot daggers at him, and simultaneously, my body reacts in a not so displeased way.

"I'm saving you," Devlin smirks, still holding on to me.

"Have you forgotten about my plus one?"

"I haven't. Have you?" He looks down at my hand, clutching the lapel of his jacket.

I jerk away from him, smoothing my hand down the front of my dress. "Unbelievable!"

"I know." Devlin grabs my hand and pulls me into the nearest closet, closing the door behind us. "There. Much better," he says.

It's dark in the tiny space, and we are too close. Thanks to the electric board, I can only see Devlin's outline, but I feel all of him. His fingers slowly brush down the side of my face, stopping with his thumb on my lips. It feels good and right.

"We shouldn't be in here," I told him.

"If you only knew what I was thinking," Devlin says, ignoring me, pulling me closer.

"I'm serious. We should go."

I should go, but my feet are planted, my body on high alert. Devlin and I are never on the same wavelength. But at this moment, it doesn't take much for me to tune into his frequency. I lean into him, even though my mind is screaming no. Even as my mouth is speaking, "We can't."

We will only end in disaster, with my heart dangling over a cliff.

Devlin traces my lips with his thumb, his tongue slipping

141

out to wet his own. "Your mouth is perfect," he says, gazing into my eyes. "You make me want to break all the rules, Eve." His brows cave in as if he's contemplating it.

My breath hitches, my heart pounding in my chest. My lips part, attempting to protest, but I can barely breathe with him touching me. He's so close I can feel his cock thickening, the pressure increasing, rising at the base of my belly.

"I can't be what you need," Devlin says, answering a question I didn't ask. "But I can be what you want right now."

"Devlin…"

*Devlin…*

Before I could finish, Devlin's mouth descended on mine. I'm caught off guard, remembering his admission that he doesn't kiss on the mouth. At that moment, I felt honored. So, I kissed him back. I hadn't realized how hungry I'd been to feel his lips on mine.

For a man who doesn't kiss, he sure does it well. With his hand gripping my hip and the other at the back of my head, Devlin gives a new meaning to the French kiss.

My toes curl to Devlin's adroit actions. My heart thumps, the blood racing through my veins. Every touch from our night together came rushing back. He gave me what I wanted then, and I haven't been able to get him off my mind since.

I wonder if he knows his effect on me—if he feels the

same ache in his chest as I do. The ache for more of everything. I fear my mind won't be the only thing at risk if we keep this up.

I can't surrender my heart too.

I can't sink deeper into the rabbit hole.

I won't.

My heart screams for me to stop, to pull away from him, and as hard as it is to do so, I listen.

I push Devlin away from me, and the tiny lights behind him spark and smoke. I reach behind me, open the door, and step into the hallway. The lights flicker in the venue before shutting off completely.

Devlin steps out after me, and the floodlights come on. I hear muffled voices from the kitchen. Unpleasantries spill down the hall toward us from the main room.

Devlin takes a step toward me, and I hold up my hand.

"Stop. Don't come any closer."

"Eve, I'm…."

"No, Devlin. You know," I said, pausing. "I'm beginning to think you're not happy unless everyone else around you is unhappy. You wear your name very well, Devil."

"What can I do to help fix this?" Devlin asks, a hint of concern on his face.

"You've done enough. Don't you think?" I tilt my head, crossing my arms over my chest angrily.

"Let me help you, Eve," his voice softens. Maybe the

softest I've ever heard him speak, but I don't believe him. I can't.

"You? *You* want to help *me*? This is your fault. None of this would be happening if it weren't for you!" I rage. "You sure know how to show a girl a good time and ruin everything else in the process."

"Eve."

I storm away from Devlin's call, straight out the back door. I'm humiliated, hurt, and a bit disappointed. A small part of me still held hope for us. That part wants to run back to him, be the rulebreaker he wants me to be. It's foolish. I know, but I'm human.

A man like Devlin can't be tamed. There's no bartering with him. He has proven himself to be disastrous over and over again. Ruining tonight was the last straw.

I pinch the bridge of my nose, trying to calm down and figure a way out of this mess.

# Chapter 16

**Devlin**

I HAVEN'T KISSED a woman in fifteen years.

It's been fifteen years since I caught my first and last girlfriend on her knees with her mouth wrapped around another man's cock.

Fifteen years I've held out, vowing my lips would never touch a woman unless she were my wife.

Fifteen years and Evelyn Parrish set my vow to flames.

I shouldn't have pulled her into the closet, but I want what I can't have. And seeing her with her plus one made me want her even more.

I hate that she's putting herself out there, dating random guys that aren't me.

She doesn't want me.

I can't have her.

We're stuck in a loop. Roadblocks are a constant between us. I usually don't mind the detours. But tonight was different. Tonight, I leaped, and though enjoyable at the moment, my spontaneity fell flat.

It was Eve's big night, what she'd wanted for years and worked so hard for months to organize, and I ruined it because of my selfish desire.

I have to fix it.

I let Eve cool off for a couple of minutes. Then, I go outside after her, leaving the chaotic voices inside. I search the rear of the venue as the sun passes the torch to the moon, but Eve is nowhere to be found. She wouldn't leave and couldn't have gone far.

I step to the side of the building, releasing a breath of relief at the sight of Eve leaning against the wall. Her head is lowered into her palms as she speaks muffled words.

Cautiously, I approach her, placing my hand on her shoulder.

"Eve," I said softly.

Eve's head snaps up, her eyes narrowing on me.

"What do you want, Devlin?" Eve asks.

I brace myself, expecting her to lash out, to throw a punch, but she just stares. Her eyes even soften a little.

"Whatever it is, I have nothing left to give you," Eve says, defeated. "I have to figure this mess out. There's no time for your games."

"Eve, I'm sorry. I want to help. No more games," I promise.

Eve gives me a questionable look.

"Let me help," I said, dropping my hand to her arm.

We may not be friends, but we make a great team. We're the best at figuring things out together. And this is mostly my fault. I won't let Eve bear the burden alone.

"Okay," Eve relents. "But this in no way excuses you. Your assistance won't make us even."

"Understood," I said.

Eve cleared her throat, face blushed but serious. "And what happened in there can never happen again." Eve points her eyes at me, waiting for a response.

I hesitate. Agreeing with Eve would be a lie. I can promise it won't happen at this venue tonight because I don't want to make things worse than they already are. But I can't tell her I won't ever kiss her again because the chance of me breaking my word is one hundred to none. Sampling her lips and never tasting them again would be torture.

"Whatever you want, Eve," I said, glancing at her lips.

Eve swallows hard again, easing her arm from my grasp. "Sawyer will be here soon. Tonight can't be a failure. So, how do you propose we handle this? Because I'm drawing a blank," she says.

"I know a guy who knows a guy," I smile. "Come on."

Eve and I walk side by side to the venue's entrance. She calls the owner to fill them in while I cash in my favor at the electric company, requesting the call from the owner is VIP'd once received.

Sarah, my favor, and her co-worker didn't waste time getting here, and the problem was fixed minutes after their arrival.

Eve and I didn't create as big a problem as we thought. Or maybe Sarah is just that good at her job.

"You know, when you said I owed you one, this isn't what I thought you had in mind," Sarah said, standing by the driver's door of her utility truck.

It's been over a year since I've seen Sarah, and this isn't exactly what I had in mind, either. I talked a guy I knew out of towing her car from an illegal parking spot late one night, and I'll just say she was grateful. But I had family dinner and couldn't stay out to play. She gave me a business card with her personal number scribbled on the back, and I never called. While contemplating, I decided against it. She seemed like the serious type, and I wasn't in a place to stick around.

I open the door for her, grinning. "Me either." I glanced behind me, where Eve stood watch at the venue's entrance. "But things change," I said, looking back at Sarah. "I appreciate this," I told her.

"It's the least I can do. If you ever want to explore your previous thoughts, you have my number," Sarah says.

I have serious issues.

Sarah is throwing herself at me, and all I can think about is the woman standing behind me, burning a hole in my back. The woman who still wants nothing to do with me.

"Good night, Sarah. Thanks again."

Sarah nods, a disappointing smile dawning on her face, and climbs into the truck.

Eve remains in the same spot when I turn around, except now her focus isn't on me, and she's not alone. Her date, Holland, is standing in front of her, too close for my comfort. He lifts his hand to her mouth, and her lips part, opening and closing over the item in his hand.

My nostrils flared as his thumb brushed the side of Eve's mouth. She seems to enjoy this guy far better than the last asshole I saw her with. He seems to be a decent guy, but it's still painful to watch them together.

As she laughs, Eve places her palm on his chest, slightly leaning into him.

I didn't realize my feet were moving until I was standing next to her.

149

Eve drops her hand to her chest, startled. "Stop sneaking up on me," she tells me.

"What would be the fun in that?" I ask, meeting her eyes.

Eve and I stare for a long moment before Holland speaks.

"Nice friends you have. You're a popular guy," he says.

My eyes flit to his, irritated by his interruption. "When I need to be," I respond.

*And I was trying so hard to tolerate you.*

I smile tensely, returning my attention to Eve. "Let me know if you need anything else," I said, touching the side of her arm.

Eve stiffens but doesn't pull away. I can feel Holland's eyes on me. I promised Eve no more games. I promised I wouldn't kiss her again while here, and I meant it. But I can't resist toying with her. And her date.

"Let me know if you need relief from distraction," I said, giving her arm a gentle squeeze. I drop my hand, nodding to Holland. "Arland," I taunt, stepping between them and walking inside.

When Sawyer and his special guests arrive thirty minutes later, everything is up and running. As usual, Susan and Jan are pitching dirty looks my way, but I ignore them.

My eyes keep traveling to Eve on the dance floor with Holland. They're moving to the upbeat tunes in the background, laughing and chatting like old friends. He doesn't inappropriately touch her, but he does lean a little too close a few times to whisper in her ear.

I hate the guy. He's too attentive to Eve. He's perfect for her, the right height, the right build. Hell, I'd probably date him if I were her. But as good as he is, he's not the one for her in my eyes because he's not me.

"Devlin," Sawyer seizes my attention near the bar minutes after his arrival. "A word," he says, tipping a flute glass to his mouth.

"About?"

"My sources tell me you bailed Evelyn out of a jam tonight. Is that true?" Sawyer asks.

"What does it matter?"

"It matters a great deal. I need to know I can count on Evelyn to fix problems on her own as you move up in the ranks," Sawyer says. "I know the two of you are close, but when you take my place, there can be no favoritism. Empires can crumble faster than they're built."

Heeding Sawyer's warning, I look around the room, wondering who his source is. Who would want to sabotage Eve? Unless it's someone who despises me, and Eve is just a pawn.

"Your source didn't relay all of the facts. I simply mended a problem that I caused," I responded.

Sawyer side-eyes me, grinning sparsely. "And what was the problem?"

The truth wouldn't be good for Eve or me, especially since Sawyer's warned me against being with her in any capacity that isn't work-related. If he's asking questions, he likely knows what the issue is. I just need to leave Eve out of the cause.

"I needed a minute." *With Eve.* "So, I went into the closest unlocked door I could find, which happened to be the electrical panel room. I stumbled. My back hit the board, and it shorted," I shrug, explaining without explaining.

It's not the whole truth, but it's the only portion Sawyer will get.

"If it's any consolation, Eve was pissed." I still remember the horrified look in her eyes. The moment I knew I had fucked up.

Sawyer nods. "Glad to know you're keeping things professional because there's something you must do together."

My interest piques, and I face Sawyer fully. Not so much lately, but Eve and I have been doing things together since she began working for him. I watch him, waiting for an explanation, and get nothing.

Sawyer faces the crowd. "Not tonight," he says, sipping from his glass again. "We'll discuss it Monday. Enjoy the party." He sets the empty glass on the bar and leaves.

How am I supposed to enjoy the party when the woman I want to enjoy it with is here with another man?

# Chapter 17

**Evelyn**

DEVLIN WATCHING ME most of the night is disturbing but also fascinating.

The blood in my veins hasn't cooled once. It's as hot as if he were physically touching me. So, I've pretended not to notice, kept my attention on Holland, and refused even the slightest glance Devlin's way.

I never thanked him for getting tonight back on track, and I probably never will. I secretly acknowledge that I was partially to blame for what happened. Devlin didn't exactly kiss himself, and he didn't force himself on me. I joined in willingly.

I was weak.

I'm always weak inside when it comes to him, and I think he knows it. But I won't let my vice be my undoing. The raw chemistry between us has to fade at some point if we keep our distance. It has to. I'm not the woman who screws her boss.

Holland's pinky flicks mine on the table as we sit people-watching. I came. I conquered. And at this point, I just want to be done. It's getting late, and the crowd is slowly dwindling. I only wish they would ebb a little faster so I can leave.

I give Charity props for her years of service. Planning was no easy feat.

"A penny for your thoughts," Holland says.

"You don't want my thoughts tonight," I said, smiling. My thoughts are struggling to remain pure.

I haven't told Holland about the kiss, that Devlin and I were the cause of all the commotion because I can hardly believe it myself. I also haven't told him about Devlin's impending promotion.

"Try me," Holland says, linking our pinkies.

I look around the space at the open ears and eyes, knowing if I spill, one of them is bound to scoop it up.

Besides, Mr. Sawyer is only a few seats away, and Devlin is on my right side. I don't know why I thought this seating arrangement was a good idea.

From the corner of my eye, I spy the back of Devlin's head. He's conversing with Mr. Sawyer and his guests, but I'm no fool. He's a multitasker, and I'm sure his ears are as peeled as everyone else's.

"Maybe later," I replied to Holland.

Devlin's leg briefly brushes mine beneath the table, jolting me. My body stiffens, eyes popping for a second.

"You alright?" Holland asks, covering my hand with his.

"I'm fine. Just caught a chill," I smile.

Devlin laughs with Sawyer and the others, and his leg brushes mine again. I want to ask if he's doing it on purpose, but I don't want the unwanted attention from everyone around us.

"You sure?" Holland asks. "You look a little flushed."

"Maybe a little irritated." I clear my throat, righting myself in the chair while discreetly knocking my knee against Devlin's leg.

Holland gently squeezes my hand. "I'm a bit tired myself. It's been quite a night."

"You don't have to stay. I could call an Uber."

"What kind of guy would I be if I left you here? We came together. We should leave together." Holland yawns.

"Don't be ridiculous. I'm not a child," I said.

"If I may," Devlin says next to me.

Holland's eyes look past me. I don't bother turning around. I can only imagine what Devlin will say next.

155

"I couldn't help but overhear," Devlin says. "I could get Eve home safely. That's if neither of you mind."

Holland glances at me, and I mouth *no*, but he doesn't seem to comprehend.

"Eve, would you mind?" Holland asks.

Either he's toying with me, or he truly is that tired.

"Go," I said. "I'll find my way home." *Without Devlin.*

Holland nods, looking at Devlin. "Keep her safe," he says as if he's passing the torch.

"She's in good hands," Devlin responds to Holland like I'm not sitting between them.

*Great. They've decided for me.*

I close my eyes and blow out a much-needed breath.

Holland stands seconds later, leaning down to press his lips to my cheek. "I'll call you tomorrow," he says. Then he's gone.

"Great guy," Devlin says after Holland leaves.

"Yeah. He is." I smile, offering no explanation.

I sat silent for the next thirty minutes as the crowd continued to thin.

Mr. Sawyer walks his guests out, and I follow them, grateful that the night is finally over.

I stop in front of the venue, pulling my phone out to call a ride when Mr. Sawyer comes to stand in front of me.

"Well done, Evelyn," Mr. Sawyer says.

"Thank you," I said.

Devlin appears at my side with his hands tucked into his pockets, and Mr. Sawyer looks at him and back to me.

"Do you need a lift home?" Mr. Sawyer asks.

I raise my phone awkwardly. "Got it covered."

Mr. Sawyer stares at me for a moment. "Nonsense," he says, his eyes moving to my right. "Devlin, make sure she gets home. And remember what I said."

"Will do," Devlin replies.

*Men.*

A few minutes later, I'm in the passenger seat of Devlin's car. Oddly, I feel like I belong here beside him. I feel safe, but that can't be right. He's a maniac. Not to be trusted with my life.

Jan's frantic explanation from earlier pops into my head, and I grin.

Devlin turns the music down. "What's so funny?" he asks.

My head swivels toward him. "You really are a piece of work, Devlin. You behave like nothing matters but you and what you want. Life doesn't work that way. You're smug and shrewd," I pause, shaking my head.

There are so many bad things I can say about him, but he's not all bad all the time. He's not bad at all. He's just a man who prefers to live a solitary life. He never claimed to be anyone else.

157

I wonder if things were different, if he were different, if he wanted more, would I still be drawn to him?

"I'm a lot more than that, Eve," Devlin says.

"You're right about that," I pause again, regretting my next words before they're spoken. "You're the most confusing man I've ever met. One moment you're hot, the next you're cold. I loathe that about you, how free you are to play with people's emotions."

"Careful, Eve. Sounds an awful lot like you're falling for me. And we can't have that. Can we?"

"Get over yourself. You make it impossible for anyone to fall for you."

"Not impossible," Devlin says. "There's a reason for everything I do."

I examine Devlin's features as he drives, his straight-lined lips and a slight tick in his jaw.

"There," I point out. "That right there."

"What?" Devlin glances at me.

"That thing you do. It's like you give a little and take it away in the next breath. Your parents must be real proud," I quipped.

"You don't know shit about my parents," Devlin bristles in a low burly tone that only serves as fuel for me to continue.

"Finally, a real, honest, human emotion."

"I've always been real with you, Eve," Devlin says, his temple joining in the beat. He grips the steering wheel, keeping his eyes forward.

"And honest?" I asked.

"I've been as honest as I needed to be. We're not dating. We're not fucking. Not anymore. And, according to you, we're not friends. So, what's there to be honest about, huh? What are you asking for? What do you want from me?"

*Wow.*

I look out the front windshield, dazed and confused by his words. My eyes burn, tears threatening, halted by my refusal to let even one slip.

What is wrong with me?

I don't cry, not even with John.

Screw Devlin and this power he has over me.

I don't know what I'm asking of him.

I don't know what I want.

I remain quiet, my breaths shallow and my heart pounding.

"Can you truly say that you've been completely transparent with me? That there's nothing you're holding back?" Devlin asks.

*No. I can't.*

I tighten my hand around my wrist on my lap to stay grounded. Only heartbreak and ruin could come from my truth. I will not tell him about the crazy possibilities haunting

159

my daydreams because he couldn't handle them. And neither could I.

"Forget it," I said. "I shouldn't have pried. If there's anything that hasn't already been said, it's for good reason." Devlin turns onto my driveway and stops in front of the garage.

I sit there staring for a moment longer than I should have. Neither of us speaks. Music hums in the background echoing the rise and fall of Devlin's chest. His finger taps his knees as his head turns toward me. My eyes locked onto his questioning gaze, complication answering loudly in my head.

"Eve," Devlin says softly, too softly, as he leans toward me. My name was rich on his lips. His voice seemed to reverberate through me, prickling my skin and warming my bones.

"Thanks for the ride," I said quickly. Nothing proper ever follows when Devlin says my name like that. "Guess I'll see you at the office."

Devlin squints his eyes for a second. Then he nods, righting himself in the driver's seat. "See you at the office," he agrees.

I leave Devlin's car with my lips pressed. I don't release them until I'm inside my home with my back against the door. The breath rushes out of me as I bend at the waist, holding my hand to my heart. I'm not sure what's happening. It never hurts so much to breathe.

How can I be lucky and unlucky at the same time?

# Chapter 18

**Devlin**

SOMETIMES I THINK Sawyer hates my guts, and other times I think he *really* hates my guts. Why else would he taunt me like this? There's only so much I can take.

I've gone out of my way to avoid Eve since taking her home after the party three months ago. I dived into work, reacquainting myself with the departments and adjusting to my new position.

And now this.

Sawyer is not an idiot. He's not blind to my attraction to Eve. I'm sure he knows the complications that may arise from this, but he insists we do it.

I rapped my knuckles on Eve's office door, hearing her voice seconds later.

"Come in."

Eve looks at me expectantly as I walk toward her.

"Got a minute?" I asked.

"Yeah. Sure, Boss," Eve smiles slyly, attempting to break the ice that's grown thick between us.

I smile over my uncertainty, sitting in the chair before her.

"Please," I said. "Formalities aren't necessary, Eve. I'm the same man I've always been."

"I think it's appropriate. Wouldn't want anyone to get the wrong idea," Eve says.

"You never struck me as someone who cared what others think."

"I don't."

"Good. Don't change who you are on my account."

"Don't worry. I won't." Eve breathes sharply. "What can I do for you, Devlin?"

"I need you to pack a bag," I said bluntly.

"What on earth for?"

I smirk, deciding to toy with her for a bit. "Because you're going away with me."

Eve's eyes widened, her back flattening to her chair. "Uhm, excuse me?"

"You heard right. We're taking a trip. Just you and me."

"The hell I am," Eve says, throwing her manners out the window. Her eyes flit around the room, around me to the door and back. "Are you recording me? What game are you playing?"

"Oh, it's not a game. Trust me. I'm just as excited about it as you are."

"Do I look excited?" Eve asks.

I want to tell her she looks nervous, angry, and on the verge of distraction, but I don't want to push my limits too far. Getting her to agree will be hard enough without further commentary from me.

"My point exactly," I responded instead. "Look, unless you're prepared to walk out that door and never look back, I'm afraid there's no other choice. You may not like it. I may not like it, but Sawyer is still our boss, and he made it clear that this trip is a must. I could go alone, but I'd prefer not to. Finding your replacement at such short notice would be taxing."

Eve's lips thinned, her nose flaring as she stared at me. I assume she's trying to refrain from chewing me out. Her elbows fold, fingers tapping hastily to the sides of her arms.

I don't want to lose her, but she seems to be considering walking out. I slide my palms down my thighs and hold my breath, anxiously awaiting her response.

"Where are we going?" Eve asks.

I release my breath. "Since Charity is still out, we have to meet with Robert at the factory in Mintville tomorrow morning. I guess Sawyer didn't think Jan could handle it alone."

Sawyer has two factories. One here in Plains, SC, and one in Mintville, NC. Twice a year, he sends the design team on an impromptu visit to check on things. Robert won't know what hit him until we're there. Hopefully, there's nothing crucial to report after our visit.

"May I ask why?" Eve eyes me curiously with her fingers on the edge of her desk.

"To spy, of course. Take a tour. Gauge moral. Inspect the products. We'll be there for two days and two nights, checking in at the factory for two to four hours daily. Think of it as a working vacation."

Talking about going away with Eve has me thinking about ways to blur the lines already. That can't be good. It's not good.

Sawyer's probably somewhere laughing, waiting for me to fuck up.

So, it's simple.

I won't.

I can and will keep my libido in check.

Eve deserves more than me.

I wonder what happened with that Holland guy she was with at the party? He was a confident one, secure enough with his manhood to trust Eve with me. He would likely be good for her, but I can't stand the idea of her with someone else.

"When do we leave?" Eve's voice breaks through my thoughts.

"Our flight leaves at six in the morning. We should arrive in Mintville around seven-thirty. Everything's taken care of."

"And we'll have separate rooms. Right?" Eve asks.

"I presume so. Sawyer had his assistant make the arrangements."

"Well then," Eve sighs. "I guess there's no excuse not to go."

I grip the arms of the chair and stand. "Guess not," I agreed, pressing my fingertips to her desk. "By the way, you'll be moving into the office next to mine when we get back."

"What's wrong with the office I have now?" Eve questions.

*It's too far away from me.*

"With the adjoining office empty, I don't see a reason to keep you here." I look back at the space separating my old office from Eve's. "Unless you've changed your mind about my replacement," I inquire.

"No," Eve says quickly. "I just didn't expect us to still be so... close."

I chuckle. "Look at it this way. At least you won't have to worry about seeing my face every time you lift your head. And I can still help you if you are in a jam."

Eve squints her eyes at me. "And Mr. Sawyer's okay with that?"

I shrug. "I didn't ask." I turn to leave, stopping when I reach the door. "One more thing," I said, holding up a finger. "Vicky and I will swing by for you in the morning. She's taking us to the airport."

"Victoria," Eve says. "I was wondering what happened to her."

I smile slyly. "Vicky's not going anywhere. She's special," I pause. "The two of you will get along nicely," I wink.

Eve opens her mouth and closes it. Her hands ring together tightly on the desk.

I knew the mention of Vicky would vex Eve. She likely thinks I'm an even bigger ass now than before, but I don't care. Watching her squirm excites me so much that I can't bear to look at her any longer with the growing bulge in my slacks.

"Be ready at five," I told Eve before I walked away, hoping she didn't notice.

EVEN AT FIVE AM, Eve is a sight for sore eyes.

I lick my lips as she walks to my car, her effortless beauty radiant in the dimly lit sky.

Vicky slaps my leg from the passenger seat. "You could've helped her with her bag, Dev."

"I could have," I said. "But I don't think she wants my help. She's still bitter about the party." Among other things.

"Who wears date attire for a plane ride this early in the morning?" Vicky asks.

"Someone going on a business trip," I answered, not taking my eyes off Eve for a second.

"Age is not making you wiser," Vicky says.

"I'm wise enough to know when to keep my distance."

"That distance is gonna cost you if you're not careful," Vicky warns.

It's already costing me—my cognitive functions, space, and time. And that's with me trying to be careful. I can only imagine if I weren't careful at all.

I get out to help Eve put her bag in the trunk once she reaches the car. *Good morning* is all that's said between us. Then we get back inside with her sitting behind Vicky.

169

I should've let Vicky drive, so I didn't have the option to glance at Eve along the way, which I did several times. But her eyes were focused outside her window the entire drive.

We're standing outside the airport when Vicky holds her hands out for my keys. Her eyes sparkle a little too much, making me nervous about trusting her with my car.

I place the keys in her hand but don't let go yet. "Not a scratch," I warned.

"It's just a thing, Dev. It can be repaired and replaced," Vicky says.

I reluctantly let go as she moves to Eve.

"You know, when Dev told me he was going away with you, I didn't believe him. I was concerned," Vicky says to Eve.

"Oh, no," Eve rushed out. "You have nothing to worry about. It's not like that. Devlin and I are not…."

"Eve," Vicky soothes. "I know. Dev is an honest man. He wouldn't hurt me," Vicky assures her. "I only meant the way he talks about your disdain for him. I didn't know if you'd survive the trip," Vicky laughs.

Eve grins softly, seeming relieved.

"Well, safe travels, and enjoy the trip. As much as you can, anyway, seeing as it's all business," Vicky wrinkles her nose. "You have my permission to go out and enjoy the city. Have fun," Vicky encourages.

"Thanks, but I doubt we'll have little time for anything but work," Eve says.

Vicky steps in front of me, her arms going around my neck, and I hug her back. "She's so into you," she whispers away from Eve's prying ears. "The boss won't be happy, but go get her tiger." She growls playfully in my ear, and I can't help but laugh. Vicky releases me, putting space between us.

"Be careful with my baby," I told Vicky.

"That car is hardly a baby," Vicky says. She looks at Eve. "Don't be too hard on him," she says, then her eyes return to me. "Text me when you land."

I nod. Then, Eve and I enter the airport separately but together.

# Chapter 19

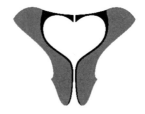

**Evelyn**

WHAT IS THIS life? My life.

It's hardly believable and mildly disappointing.

I'm going away with Devlin. Yet, it's not the kind of going away I would have imagined.

We just left his… Victoria outside the airport an hour ago. I'm not sure what she is to him at this point. I was jealous of their hug, envious of the smile she brought to his face, but grateful a kiss didn't ensue. They're not overly affectionate, but maybe that's one of Devlin's rules too. No

173

explicit PDA. Victoria seems okay with being a *buddy*, and her confidence is through the roof. No worries at all about Devlin and me. But I guess that's one of the perks of being as beautiful as she is, compared to myself.

"Aisle or window?" Devlin lifts my carry-on into the overhead compartment.

I jerk my eyes away from the hard lines in Devlin's arms. Unlike me, he didn't pre-dress for our meeting. His pecs stretch against his soft T-shirt, the tail rising, revealing an imprint in his jeans below his waist.

"Huh?"

Devlin smiles, catching me in the act, and I blush.

"Aisle or window?" He asks again.

"Window," I answered, stepping past the aisle seat.

Devlin eyes me closely as he sits next to me as if he can see straight through me. I know what he's thinking, but I'm not distracted. Well, maybe a little, but it can't be helped. Not by him.

Devlin leans close to my ear. "Are you not a fan of flying?" He asks.

*I'm not a fan of flying with you.*

My body reacts, heating immediately to his proximity. I turn my head toward him, our lips nearly brushing.

"I'll be fine. I don't favor takeoffs," I explained, smiling with the half-truth.

Concern shows on Devlin's face. "Don't worry. I'll be here the entire time."

*That's what I'm afraid of.*

I stare into his eyes, reading more into his words than I should.

I'm afraid of my weakness for him. I'm concerned that if Devlin tries, really tries to claim me, I won't be able to stop him. I'm sick, and my drug is the cause and cure.

Minutes later, the plane rushes the runway, and I clutch the armrests for dear life, my eyes covered in darkness. My stomach dips as gravity gives way to the plane. I press my feet firmly to the floor, my lips moving as I silently recite a prayer.

Warmth covers my hand. A gentle squeeze follows as the seconds pass, comforting, reassuring. For a few seconds, I'm reminded that I'm not alone.

When the plane levels, I open my eyes and look at Devlin's hand secure on mine. Our eyes meet, sincerity in his, caution in mine. It takes my mind off one fear and throws it into another.

*I'm glad it's you who holds my hand.*

*I'm terrified it's you who holds my hand.*

Still, I allow him to remain there until he's ready to let go because I don't want him to.

"Better now?" Devlin asks, his hand still on me.

"Yes. Thanks."

175

"It was my pleasure," Devlin says, and my fingers twitch beneath his. "How do you feel about landings?" he asks, his lips tilting into a smile.

I jerk my hand away, scorning myself for the temporary lapse. I'd almost forgotten who Devlin is, that he's incapable of being serious with anyone.

"I'll manage," I snapped.

"Well, if you change your mind," Devlin says, showing me his hand.

*I won't.*

A sarcastic grunt escaped me. I look away without voicing my thoughts, resting my head on the seat and focusing on the clear blue sky until my eyelids are too heavy to keep open.

"ARE YOU A member of the mile-high club, Eve?" Devlin asks.

I stare at him like he's lost his damn mind.

"So, that's a no," he chuckles. "Damn shame. I think you'd enjoy it," he says.

"Is that a dare?" I squint my eyes at him.

"No. But if you're considering, it could be a promise." Devlin's teeth rake across his bottom lip as his eyes roam over me.

"A promise of what?" I laugh, sobering quickly at his gaze.

"A promise of a lifetime membership with unlimited access."

I cough, my spit lodged in my throat. I'm unsure if Devlin is offering himself up or simply stating I should try it with someone else.

I feel dared.

I'm intrigued.

"With you?" I asked.

"Who else?" Devlin glances around the plane. "It has to be me, Eve," he says seriously, rubbing his thumb over the back of my hand.

I'm concerned he's the only man for the job, the only one who'd make the risk worth my while.

"If I agreed—and I'm not saying I do, but if I did—what happens next?" I asked.

"I'd start with a touch here," Devlin says, grazing my thigh with his palm. "And a tease here." His thumb traces the outline of my lips.

In a flash, Devlin is kneeling before me, drawing my panties down my thighs.

"What are you doing?" I whisper-shout, my fright instincts kicking in.

I don't remember saying yes, but I must have because this feels like something I desire. The only thing that gives me pause is the eyes watching us across the aisle.

"People are watching," I said, catching the eyes of the man next to us.

"All the more reason to continue." Devlin parts my thighs. "Let me liberate you, Eve. Let me taste you. Let them watch," he says, hiking my dress higher.

My pussy clenched at his words. I crane my neck back at the force of his tongue, flicking my clit, and again, I don't remember saying yes.

But, "Yes." I cry out, leaning into Devlin's mouth, wanting more, craving more. I revel in the dips, the precise movements of his tongue, and just as I near the edge, he stops and looks at me.

"Why'd you stop?" I ask frantically, attempting to pull his head back into position.

"Because I want you to remember this. How I make you feel. Remember who's in control. I have the power to give you what you want and the power to take it away. I'm in control, Eve."

"Fine," I breathe. "You're in control. Now, finish it," I demanded.

Devlin reclaims my pussy, pushing his thumb inside me, sucking my clit, spurring my need to feel him deeper, harder, faster. He complies, his finger diving, massaging my walls, his tongue stimulating.

I rock my hips to his rhythm, feeling the buildup once more. "Damn you, Devlin," I moaned.

Devlin answers, a low murmur coasting over me as he allows my release. As I climax, I pull his face to me, and he devours every drop.

Devlin lifts his head meeting my foggy gaze, and holds his thumb to my lips.

"Taste how sweet you are," he says.

I pause for a moment before my lips wrap around his finger, and I begin sucking it.

"That's it," Devlin coaxes. "It's hard to resist the nectar."

In the next breath, I'm on my knees, propped between Devlin's legs, with my lips sliding up and down his shaft, my tongue coasting over the barely-there vessels in his cock.

"That's it, Eve," Devlin says again.

I continue, my head bobbing and hand mimicking the motion at the base of his dick. My pussy pulses as if Devlin is filling me. I want him inside me, but I want to feel him erupt in my mouth more.

People on the plane are standing now, quietly enjoying the show, but I don't care. I'm in control now. I want him to feel what I felt.

Devlin's hand touches the back of my head, urging me on.

"Eve," he says, his head drifting backward.

"Eve," he whispers, closing his eyes.

"Eve," he grunts, his hips jerking onto my face.

"Fuck, Eve," he shouts, gripping the hair behind my head and pumping his dick into my mouth.

I close my eyes, sucking urgently. The harder I suck, the further away Devlin's voice seems to be. Gooey warmth plummets the back of my throat, and I swallow, continuing my movements until he's spent.

"Eve," Devlin whispers so softly I barely hear him.

I crane my eyes open, smiling, satisfied that he knows who's boss. But it's not Devlin's eyes I see staring back at me.

# Chapter 20

**Devlin**

I WISH I COULD freeze time and live in this moment with Eve. She snuggled into my side a few minutes ago, and I allowed her to remain. She seemed content with her hand on my abs and her head on my chest. Maybe too content with our surroundings. I love the sounds she makes, but I'd prefer it if her moans were reserved for only me.

"Eve."

I slide my thumb over her mouth, and her lips part, her tongue slithering out to tease the tip of my finger. She grabs my hand, pushing my thumb into her mouth.

"Eve."

I try to free my thumb, but she won't let go. She sucks it as if it pacifies her.

I glance at the people next to us, smiling awkwardly. The guy looks intrigued while the woman wears a face of disgust.

I can only imagine how this must look, a grown woman sucking my thumb while she sleeps. They probably think Eve and I are into some weird kink, which I don't have a problem with if it's what she's into. I would do just about anything she asked if we were alone.

"Eve."

She sucks gently, then harder, and gently until her mouth stills.

"Eve."

She moans again and smiles.

*Beautiful.*

I stare as her eyes open. My dick hardens as her eyes widen. I try to think it down, but it's no use when my finger is still in her mouth, wet and warm. If this is the treatment she gives a finger; I can only imagine what other tricks her mouth can do.

Eve jerks away from me, her eyes intent and full of rage. "What's the matter with you?" She asks as if I'm the one who forced my thumb into her mouth.

"I was just about to ask you the same thing." I lift a brow. "Wet dream?" I ask.

Eve's nose flares. "You're disgusting."

I wiggle my thumb in front of her. "You sure about that?"

"I'm pretty sure if I had a…." Eve paused, looking around the plane. Then, she leans in, whispering. "If I had a wet dream, you'd be nowhere near it." She backs away again.

"By the way, you're welcome."

"I don't remember thanking you," Eve says.

I shrug. "Maybe you should."

"For what, exactly?"

"Letting you use me. I've never had foreplay quite like that. Your delivery was superb." I pause, leaning away from prying ears. "Just tell me one thing. Was the guy as satisfied as you made him out to be?"

"Screw you, Devlin," Eve says quietly.

"Tsk, tsk, Eve. Be careful what you ask for. You just might get it," I said, winking at her.

Something about being trapped on a plane with Eve not being able to escape spars me to continue even though I know it's wrong.

I was on my best behavior until Eve did what she did. Now, I can't stop the words from spilling out of my mouth. I can't bury the emotions any longer. She unleashed the wicked, and I don't know if I can put him back in the box. Truthfully, I don't want to.

"You're so full of it," Eve says.

"I'm not the one lying to myself."

*Not anymore.*

I want Eve in my life, whatever that may mean. The more time I spend with her, the more certain I am. There's something brewing between us. When we're apart, it smolders, getting stronger. And when we're together, the intensity is almost too much to bear.

I address the watchers next to us. "You'll have to excuse my wife. She gets nervous on planes."

The guy clears his throat, leaning forward from the window seat. "You're a lucky man," he says boldly.

"I am," I agreed.

Eve and the woman across the aisle seem to be on the same wavelength. Their elbows connected with our sides at the same exact moment.

"What? It was a compliment," the guy says to the woman.

"Let's see how lucky you are," she replied.

"I am not your wife," Eve says as I face her.

"No. You're not. But I am a lucky man," I said quietly.

Eve looks out the window, spouting words under her breath. I can always sense when she's had enough, usually when she shuts down and gives me the last word like now.

I remain quiet, giving Eve space until the pilot announces that we'll be landing soon.

ROBERT WAS SURPRISED when Eve and I arrived but not unprepared. He runs a tight ship, and his employees seem to be happy. Or, they're very good at pretending. Supplies are stocked. Production is on schedule, and the products are ninety-eight percent perfection. Not even machines are fault free.

"I'm surprised Charity couldn't make the trip herself," Robert says.

I look at Eve speaking with an employee a few feet away. It's hard to keep my eyes off her. She's even more distant since the plane ride. She's barely looked at me all morning.

"Charity is out on medical leave. Maybe next time she'll feel up to it," I told Robert.

"How long has Evelyn been with the company?" Robert asks.

I turn to face him, curious why he wants to know but keep the jealousy to myself. "It's been years. I don't let her out much," I joked.

Robert grins. "Is she seeing anyone?" he asks with his eyes on Eve.

I like Robert, but he's barking up the wrong tree.

"I believe so. Some guy back home last I heard." Though, I'm not sure if that's true. Eve hasn't mentioned

Holland since the party last year. Even so, I'd say anything to deter Robert.

"Between you and me, is it serious?" Robert asks.

My bad side welcomes Robert with open arms. I want to clip his tongue and gouge his eyes so he doesn't see or speak of Eve again.

"I shouldn't comment on employees' personal lives. Maybe you should ask her," I suggested instead.

"Of course," Rober says. "How long is your visit?"

"We'll stop by here again tomorrow. Then, we fly out Sunday morning."

"We should have dinner tonight, the three of us," Robert says, glancing at Eve.

"Sounds like a plan, but let me run it by Eve first."

"Sure," Robert agrees.

"Excuse me," I said to Robert.

I walk toward Eve, greeting the woman she's speaking with when I stop beside her.

"Mind if I steal Eve for a moment?" I asked the woman.

"Not at all, Sir," the woman croons.

I guide Eve away a few feet. She seems nervous in my presence, refusing to give eye contact.

"Do you have dinner plans?" I asked.

Eve finally looks at me. "If you count room service."

"Are you married to that plan?"

"Why, Devlin? What's this about?"

186

"Will you go out with me?" I asked casually, like we would be the only two in attendance.

ANGELA K PARKER

# Chapter 21

**Evelyn**

I CHOKE ON A LAUGH so hard that my eyes mist. I have to hold Devlin's arm to remain standing. I swear his balls grow by the second.

How could he ask me that?

After what happened on the plane, a date with Devlin is the last thing I need. I can barely look at him, much less sit for a whole meal.

"I'm sorry," I said, trying to calm down once reality dawned that everyone was staring at us. I drop my hand to my side. "You expect me to go on a date with *you*?"

Devlin smiles, but I can sense his offense. "It's not that far-fetched, Eve. There's nothing wrong with coworkers

189

sharing a meal on a business trip. And no, I don't expect anything. I only wanted to see your reaction," he says smugly. "It's not a date. Robert invited us to dinner," he explains.

For some reason, that offer appeals to me even less. Robert is a nice guy, but he won't stop staring at me. Dinner would be awkward for sure, but I'd feel like a coward if I didn't go.

"Count me in," I said.

Devlin stares as if he wants to add something more. "Okay. Well, I'll let Robert know before we leave," he says, throwing his thumb over his shoulder—the same thumb I consumed on the plane. "How much more time do you need here?" He asks.

Devlin and I came straight here after checking into the hotel this morning. He was right. We're in separate rooms, but they're adjoined. It's now lunchtime, and there's a ham and cheese sandwich on the room service menu with my name on it. We've been here long enough.

"Ten minutes, then we can go," I answered. We'll check in again tomorrow, but I don't want to leave Helen on red until then.

Devlin gives me a weird, confused look.

"Are you okay?" I asked.

"Yeah. Yeah," Devlin repeats. "Ten minutes," he says as he turns to leave.

IF I KEPT A DIARY, tonight would be titled *Dinner With a Tease and a Flirt.*

I knew what to expect from Devlin, but Robert... He's a bit much out of the office. He opened every door, pulled out my chair, offered to spread a cloth napkin over my lap, and made sure I ordered first. I suppose it wouldn't be a red flag if we were dating, but we're not. He's annoying, too eager, and plain out, trying too hard to win the attention of someone he'll likely never see again. Meanwhile, Devlin seems to be amused by my subtle frustration. I hate that he knows me so well.

"Would you like anything for dessert, Evelyn?" Robert asks, casually placing his hand over mine on the table.

I cut my eye at Devlin, covering his mouth with a napkin and pretending to wipe, but I'm onto him. There's no mistaking the curve of his lips or the mischief in his eyes.

I gulped, twisting my neck to look at Robert, and slid my hand away. I checked the invisible watch on my arm and answered, "No, thanks. It's getting late. I think I'll call it a night, but if Devlin wants to...."

"I'm going to head out too. I'm still drained from the flight," Devlin cuts in. His knee brushed mine beneath the table.

I don't dare look at him. I close my eyes for a moment, feeling the true meaning of his words to my core. I've never been so weary after a flight. I can only hope my blush isn't noticeable and, if so, that Robert doesn't think it's because of him.

Robert insists on paying the bill. Then, he drops Devlin and me off at the hotel.

Devlin and I ride the elevator to the fourth floor, and he escorts me to my room.

"Goodnight," I said, holding the keycard to the door. The lock clicks, and I push the handle down to open the door.

"I could come inside and make sure it's safe if you'd like," Devlin offers.

I pause with the door half opened, considering his offer for a few seconds.

*What happens in Mintville....*

I shake the thought away. It's safer if Devlin remains on the opposite side of my door.

"I'll take my chances," I told him.

Devlin's finger brushes my neck as he sweeps the hair over my shoulder. "Sweet dreams, Eve."

I glance over my shoulder, then disappear inside.

I practically run to the bathroom to splash my face with cold water to lessen the heat. I dip a cloth under the stream, ringing it and dabbing my neck, but it does little to dispel the warmth storming my veins. So, I shower, removing some heat and leaving the visions intact.

I pull the shower cap off my head once I'm dry and slip on a robe, compliments of the hotel. Then, I turn the TV on to drown out the silence.

An hour later, I'm fully invested in a movie about a guy who impulsively marries a woman in Vegas, only to find out she's a psycho. I gripped the pillow to my chest as she lunged for him and nearly jumped out of my skin, hearing a knock at the adjoining door.

I ignore it, knowing who's on the other side. No one knocks on a woman's door this late unless they're hurt or looking to get laid. I'd be the last person Devlin would seek out if he were hurt.

The knock comes again. I suck my teeth and roll my eyes, pressing pause on the remote. Standing, I secure the robe around me and answer the door.

"Yes," I said, annoyance rolling off me until I got a good look at Devlin's bare chest peeking between the deep slit in his robe. I swallow, moving my eyes to his.

Devlin's mouth twitched. "You weren't answering your phone," he says.

I glanced back, reminded that I'd put it on vibrate during dinner. "Yeah, sorry about that. I forgot to turn up the volume. Everything's fine."

Devlin looks over my shoulder. "Mind if I watch it with you?"

I furrowed my brows. "The movie?"

Devlin shrugs. "Sure. Why not?"

"Are you sure? It's not that good," I lied.

"Then, maybe it will help lull me." He rubs the back of his neck, his voice void of sarcasm. He does look restless, his eyes a light shade of red.

I'm already kicking myself inwardly, but I give in. "Okay, but the bed is off limits."

"Fine by me," Devlin says as I step aside to let him in. He sits in the chair next to the bed, focusing on the screen like he's interested.

I leave the door open and resume my position, turning the movie back on.

Minutes later, I clutch the pillow again as the woman dives for the guy a second time. "Watch out," I warned, but it was too late. She hits his head with a frying pan, knocking him out cold.

Devlin snorts quietly, drawing my attention. I had been pretending he wasn't there, and he's been quiet until now. His head lolls to one side, and I realize it's the first time I've witnessed him asleep. He was telling the truth, after all. His peace brings a smile to my face. He truly is a handsome man, even more so when unconscious.

I refocus on the movie, finding the ending quite disturbing. The woman killed her husband and fled without consequence.

Devlin still sleeps peacefully with his head in the same uncomfortable position. My neck hurts for him.

I stand and go to Devlin, bringing the pillow with me. Placing it behind him, I ease his head onto it. I don't have the heart to wake him. I feel safe with him here, not enough to offer space in my bed, but enough to want him close. I can't deny that I feel something other than contempt for him, but it's too late to do anything about it now. Our time has passed. He is my boss.

My fingertips barely brush the tips of Devlin's hair near his ear, and he stirs, his head moving from one side to the other. He slouches a little, dropping his hand between his legs, gripping and releasing his dick over the thick robe.

"Mmm," Devlin moans.

I pull away as if I'm prying on a private moment. I should wake Devlin up and send him back to his room. I lift my hand, stopping before I touch his shoulder.

"No. Let him sleep," I said, moving toward the bed.

"Eve," Devlin whispers behind me.

I freeze, scared to turn around, afraid of what I'll see, what Devlin will do, but most of all, terrified that I won't be able to contain myself—That we'll end up wrapped in each other's arms with bare bodies and open hearts.

"Eve," Devlin says again.

I release a deep breath and turn to find him still asleep. Relief covers me, and my ego swells, knowing it's me he's dreaming of. I get into bed, deciding to let him sleep, curious if he says anything more, but he doesn't.

My eyelids start to feel heavy after a few minutes of watching Devlin, so I relent.

# Chapter 22

**Devlin**

I INTENDED TO LEAVE when I woke up this morning, but Eve was tossing in her sleep. Whatever dream she's having is not the good kind. I couldn't leave her. So, I stayed and watched.

I thought about joining Eve in bed after she'd settled a little, being the big spoon to her frame—a frame that fits so well within mine, but decided against it when her head moved from side to side.

"No," Eve says, shaking her head. Her hands fist at her side. "Please, don't," she shouts.

I sit on the side of the bed, unsure if she'll lash out if I touch her. I place a timid hand on her shoulder, keeping my face away from her hands, just in case.

"Eve," I whispered her name once, twice, three times, and a fourth before she responded.

Eve inhaled sharply as her eyes popped open and her back bowed off the bed. She jerks to a seated position, frantically searching the room until her eyes settle on me. Her arms fly around my neck, and I hesitate, my body as confused as my mind. Shallow breaths coat my neck as she buries her face there. Her heartbeats race against my chest. Sensing she needs comfort, I hug her back, and she relaxes onto me.

I rub Eve's back, wishing I could erase the horror in her mind. "I'm here, Eve. I'm here," I coaxed. "It was just a dream."

Eve rests a few seconds longer before pulling away. I want to draw her back to me, lie next to her, and continue to comfort her, but the moment has passed. I see in her eyes that she's fully awake and possibly regretting every second since she woke.

I try not to notice the opening in her robe revealing half her breast, but it's impossible to ignore.

I clear my throat, nodding toward the opening. "You may want to…."

Eve glances down. "Oh," she says, shoving the robe closed. "Thanks."

"I know you said the bed was off limits, but you looked like you needed to be rescued."

"Yeah, sorry about that. Must've been the movie," Eve explains.

"No need for apologies. I'm glad I could help."

I search Eve's eyes, wishing I could do and say more, but think better of it. I want to be that guy who does and says all the right things for her. I just don't know how to keep a conversation on the right track. I always veer off and end up at the wrong station.

I stand, feeling my need for her grow.

"Now that you're okay, I'll go," I said, walking toward the joint door. "Let me know when you're ready," I said over my shoulder.

Eve responds by closing the door behind me.

Two hours later, Eve and I are stepping through the factory doors, greeted by Robert.

"I'm usually off on Saturday due to the short hours, but for you," Robert smiles, pointing his eyes at Eve first, then me.

I thought he would have taken the hint by now, but he hasn't. Even I recognized Eve's dismissal time and time again, and it wasn't directed at me.

"You didn't have to come in on our account. We know our way around, and we'll only be an hour," I told Robert.

Eve's head snapped toward me, and she smiled as if saying thank you. We had agreed on two hours, but I think we've seen all we need to see. I make a note to ask her if she wants to file a report against him when we return home. I want to file a report against him for testing my patience by flirting with Eve. He doesn't know when to give up. I wonder if he's that way with any of his employees. I'll have to dig deeper into that.

"It's all part of management," Robert replies.

Silence fills the air as I wait for Robert to disappear, but he remains. So, I spell it out for him in a way he should understand. Eve and I don't need a babysitter.

"Eve and I are going to do one more walk-through. We'll stop by your office on our way out."

The smile drops from Robert's face. "Oh. Okay, I'll see you then," he says, fazed.

I follow Eve's lead as we talk with a few more employees and watch others in action. It was fascinating witnessing ideas drawn on paper be born.

There was one concern that didn't come up yesterday, and I suppose a key reason why Robert didn't want to let us out of his sight. An employee disclosed she hadn't received a raise in two years, which means someone been pocketing the money. I haven't been in my position long, but

I know that all of Sawyer's businesses are uniform, and all employees should be reviewed yearly and compensated accordingly. The only way you don't get a raise is if you're fired for not doing your job. It's one more thing I'll have to report back on.

When Eve and I are done, we stop by Robert's office to say goodbye, maybe forever, once the issues are addressed.

"Did you find everything okay?" Robert asks, crossing his arms over his chest and tapping his feet on the floor. He seems nervous. His entire attitude toward Eve has shifted.

"We learned a lot. You have a great team here. You should value that," Eve responds, teasing the issue without giving it away.

I shake Robert's hand because it's the norm to conclude business dealings. "I'll be in touch," I told him.

Eve is quiet in the rental car on the way back to the hotel. She faces front in the elevator ride to our room, not sparing a single glance my way.

I stand behind her, wondering what she is thinking about, whether she's afraid to be alone with me. Trying to keep my hands to myself and stay in my corner, stealing glances, and harboring wishes is a task.

Robert comes to mind just as the elevator opens, and I compare the two of us. But I'm nothing like him. Am I? Sure, I flirt with Eve every chance I get, but she's never given me the creeped-out look she gave Robert.

Still, that doesn't make it right. It makes it worse now that I'm her boss.

As we exit the elevator, I make a conscious decision to be less invasive when it comes to Eve.

I stop next to Eve as she opens her door, and she looks at me expectantly.

"You wanna come inside?" She asks.

*Yes. Yes, I want to come inside.*

Why did Eve wait until I decided to turn over a new leaf to invite me in?

"No," I answered.

Eve's forehead wrinkles.

"I shouldn't," I said, pausing, talking the demon off my shoulder. "I'm gonna go. You know where I am if you need anything."

I walk away to escape that look on Eve's face. It's confusing. I hear Eve's door close behind me when I reach my room.

Once inside, I look at the fridge. My mind travels a hundred miles per second. I'm not the type to get wasted, but if ever there was a perfect time, it's now. Our plane doesn't leave until morning. I'd have plenty of time to sober up.

I think about Eve in the next room and how easy it would be to gain access. On second thought, maybe drinking isn't the best idea. I'd end up knocking on Eve's door again, and she would let me in. There would be a lot more than sleep and nightmares happening.

I pace the floor, stopping to gaze out the window into the woods behind the hotel. I stare for a few minutes, then pace some more before sitting in the chair by the bed. I grab the menu from the bedside dresser, browsing the selection.

Moments later, a knock sounds at the door. Looking over, I answer, "Come in." I'd left it unlocked this morning in case Eve needed me.

I remain seated, barely glancing Eve's way when she enters. My heartbeats quicken. She's in my domain. My eyes connecting with any part of her could be dangerous at the moment.

Eve comes closer, stopping at the foot of the bed. "I see we had the same idea," she grins.

"Yeah," I said, focused on the menu.

Eve rounds the bed, stopping in front of me. Seconds of silence pass between us.

"Are you okay," She asks.

I flip the page, answering, "Yes, why do you ask?"

"You seem different since we got back." Eve clears her throat. "And you haven't looked at me once since I got here."

I drop the menu onto the dresser and look at Eve. "There's a reason for that."

"Oh," Eve inquires.

203

I stare into her eyes, wondering why she's here. What game is she playing? She wants me to look at her now? Why is she dressed like that in my room, taunting me with her Cami and lace-trimmed shorts? She looks ready for a lot more than bed.

*Fuck my luck.*

I swallow hard, gripping the arms of the chair, but remain silent.

As I watch Eve, my choices hit me hard. Either I let her go or go all in. I'm not sure I can let her go when the thought of her with anyone else feels like torture. But what do I do when the obvious choice is more terrifying than the alternative?

"It's clear you want to be left alone. I'm gonna go," Eve says, turning her back to me and taking a few steps.

"Wait," I speak up, standing.

Eve stops, and I walk up behind her, leaving a slither of space between us.

"Looking at you makes it hard to hold boundaries. I've drawn so many lines, Eve. So many I've lost count." I trail a finger over her shoulder.

Eve faces me, her soft eyes meeting mine, and I wish she had kept her back to me.

"The problem is, when I look at you, I cross them all. It's like nothing else matters but the moment we're in. You make me want to say fuck it all, Eve." My finger moves down her arm to her hand.

Eve sucks in a breath, speechless. Her eyes dart toward the window as her fingertips twitch against mine.

"So, why the sudden urge to stop looking?" Eve asks.

"Robert," I said.

Eve looks at me. "Robert?"

I nod. "I noticed how uncomfortable you were around him, and it got me thinking. I don't want you to feel that way about me. I've been unfair to you," I admit.

"You haven't...."

"Yes. I have. Circumstances have changed, and I don't want you to feel like you have to accept my actions because of my position. I may not always show it, but I respect you, Eve. You deserve more than I've given you, and that changes now."

"Right now?" Eve asks.

"Yes."

"So, no more looks or dirty talk?"

"That's right."

Eve steps close to me, her chest barely touching mine. "Are you sure?" She asks, linking her fingers through mine. "Because I'm distracted, and you said...."

"I know what I said, but it's not right. We shouldn't." I don't believe my words. I don't believe Eve. She must've

205

had a bottle before she came over. "Have you been drinking?"

Eve laughs. "No, but all your talk about how we shouldn't makes me want to do something other than run away. I know things have changed, but we haven't. I'm still Eve, and you're still Devil," Eve hints a smile. "Watching you handle Robert was something. It may have skewed my view of you."

"What's gotten into you?" I asked. She's not the Eve I know. Or maybe I don't know her as well as I thought I did. Not that I'm complaining. It's not the worst side of her. She just appeared at the most inopportune time.

Eve stares at me as if I should already know the answer. She drops her hands and walks to the window, peering outside.

"Don't worry. This isn't a trap or a plea. It's an offer that we can both agree on and benefit from. One final hurrah," Eve says, glancing over her shoulder and back. "Or not," She shrugs, hugging herself.

My eyes trickle over Eve's backside from head to feet. I can't believe I'm considering her offer after my effort to talk myself out of pursuing her. She's got a hold on me that I can't break.

"I haven't been transparent with you, Devlin," Eve continues. "I'm attracted to you in a way that I haven't been with anyone else, and I need to get over it if we're to continue working together. I hope admitting my truth dulls this thing between us, and if you agree... If we do this, I hope it helps us move on."

Eve can't be thinking clearly. How is fucking her going to help me move on? It would only heighten the blow.

I walk up behind her, unable to stand the distance any longer. I give in to my urge, touching the side of her arms and breathing her in. Her skin is just as I remembered it, smooth, soft, radiant.

I can't stop wanting Eve because the rules have changed.

I could argue technically that Eve and I are not at work. We're not in a relationship, and I'm not the one seducing her. It's the opposite.

Eve could argue that I'm non-compliant and an unreasonable employer if I don't satisfy her needs.

They're both compelling arguments, but it's not that simple.

I conclude that I can't deny Eve, and I can't break the rules, but it wouldn't hurt to bend them.

I tip my mouth to Eve's ear, dropping a hand to her hip. "I won't fuck you, Eve, but make no mistake, I'm still your number one. If it's relief you need, it's my duty to please you," I said, pulling her earlobe into my mouth.

Eve whimpers, her arm tightening around her belly.

"Tell me, Eve. I need to hear you say the words.

# Chapter 23

**Evelyn**

THE SECOND DEVLIN'S tongue swept my earlobe, my confidence shrunk, and every part of me became aware of him. I can't say the words I need to say to get what I want.

"Speak it, Eve, and I'll deliver," Devlin says.

"I... I... Relieve me," I said.

A low growl escapes Devlin as the tip of his nose trails down my neck. His lips press my shoulder for a few seconds. I don't know how he's holding it together when I'm barely standing.

"What do you want for lunch?" Devlin asks.

I can't think with him so close.

"Anything," I answered.

"What's your favorite fruit?

*Fruit. Fruit.*

It seems like the hardest question at the moment.

"Blueberries," I answered.

"Mmm, I like blueberries." Devlin kisses the space behind my ear. Then the air around me chills at the loss of him.

*What the hell?*

I turn as Devlin walks to the nightstand and picks up the phone. He winks, then places an order.

I expect Devlin to prowl or gloat when he hangs up, but he surprises me by turning on some mood music on TV. He's taking our last hurrah seriously, and I'm freaking out inside. I feel like it's my first time all over again.

"Should I come back when you're ready? When lunch arrives?" I asked a few minutes later.

Devlin smiles from where he stands by the bed. Neither one of us has moved since he made the call.

"Relax, Eve. If you change your mind, we can just have lunch. It's all about you. The power is yours," Devlin says.

I paste a smile, not feeling very powerful.

"I haven't changed my mind. I just don't want to make things more awkward."

Our eyes move to the door when a knock sounds.

My eyes dart around the room to the adjoined doorway, preparing to flee until they leave.

"Don't, Eve," Devlin reads my mind. "You don't ever have to hide when you're with me. Whether we're in a crowded room or alone, there's no shame, no regret," he says.

*Why are you being so sincere?*

I adore this side of Devlin; still cocky and take charge but sweet, caring, and considerate.

Maybe....

No. Nope. There is no maybe. This is it, my system cleanse. Then we can go back to work and pretend that it never happened.

The delivery guy's eyes land on me when Devlin opens the door. I feel like he knows what's about to go down, like he knows we're about to color outside the lines.

"My wife is beautiful, isn't she?" Devlin asks the guy as he enters.

The guy nods, a blush staining his cheeks. "Yes, sir."

Devlin has a way with words, still.

I smile appreciatively, containing my shock. I just remembered I'm barely dressed, and it's the second time Devlin has referred to me as his wife. It does have a nice ring, but he's not the marrying kind, and apparently, neither am I.

The guy unloads the trays, all but one, and leaves the cart. Devlin tips him as he leaves.

"Let's eat," Devlin says, motioning to the table.

We sit across from one another as we eat a grilled cobb salad with toast.

"Tell me something no one knows about you, Eve," Devlin says suddenly.

I tear off a piece of bread. "Are we sharing now, getting personal?" I ask over a grin, popping it into my mouth. Devlin and I never shared personal details. We stick to the basics.

"Not if you don't want to."

I swallow, deciding to give him something he won't know what to do with. "Well, I've never been in love."

"What about John?" Devlin asks.

I shrug. "I loved him, but not the way one loves if they're planning a life together." Thinking about John is ruining my mood. Being the center of Devlin's attention is hard and pleasing at the same time. "What about you? Have you ever been in love?"

"No, but the idea is growing on me," Devlin says, staring into my eyes.

I imagine his words were meant for me for a moment. Could Devlin love anyone but himself? Is there a world where he could fall in love with me? I drop my eyes, forking my salad and popping it in my mouth. No. He's just speaking hypothetically.

A laugh bubbled out of me.

"What?" Devlin asks.

"Nothing. Just thinking about *you* in love."

Devlin chuckles. "Hard to imagine, but even I can change. I do have a heart, you know. It just needs a little dusting."

"A little dusting?" I raise an eyebrow.

Devlin chuckles. "And a rinse," he adds.

"I would love to see that happen," I blurted out. My smile drops as Devlin watches me. "I didn't mean it as a bad thing, only that it would be good for you to let someone in." Good for him. Bad for me. Thinking of him with anyone else leaves a bad taste in my mouth.

"Keep your eyes peeled, and you may get your wish. Things happen fast when you're open to receiving them," Devlin says.

Again, his words feel as if they're meant for me, but they can't be when he's pulling away.

Devlin tilts his head slightly. "I'm curious. Arland, that guy from the party. What's the deal with you two?"

I laugh because I'm sure Devlin knows he misquoted the name. But, I'm also curious why he wants to know.

"His name is Holland," I said, finishing the last of my salad.

"Arland, Holland. Same difference."

"Are you worried about me? Because I know you're not jealous." I set my fork down and wiped my mouth.

"You can take care of yourself, Eve. That's clear. And I may not be your man, but I care about you. I would never let anyone hurt you. You deserve greatness. I only want to know if your guy is living up to my standards."

"Your standards?"

"Yes. Does he treat you the way you should be treated? Does he protect and respect your mind, body, and soul?"

Devlin's words floor me. How could he say things like that and expect me to take it with a grain of salt? His words aren't ordinary. They're endearing. I'm more confused now than ever.

I clear my throat, pressing my back to the chair. "You don't have to worry. Every part of me is safe. Holland and I are not together, but he does look out for me. He's my best friend."

Devlin seems to relax with my confession. "Best friend?" he questions.

"Yes."

"And you've never…."

"No," I answered quickly. "I could never. We grew up together. Our relationship is pure innocence."

"Makes more sense now," Devlin says.

"What?"

"Holland sending you home with me at the party. If you were mine, I…." Devlin paused, his words lost, but he doesn't have to continue for me to know what he'd do.

214

If I were his, he never would've left me behind. He would've fallen asleep at my side before leaving me in the hands of another man. Still, it wouldn't hurt to hear him say it.

"You'd do what?" I asked.

Devlin's eyes darken, his gaze deepening into mine. "You already know," he says, standing and circling the table to stand behind me. He places his hands on my shoulders, massaging me gently.

I round my head from one side to the other, enjoying the feel of Devlin's hands on me. I wonder if there's anything he's not good at. I had forgotten about our agreement until now. I'm unsure if I can still go through with it without the potential of being hurt. My heart isn't beating down his door, but it is open after our talk.

I shove my feelings deep inside me, compartmentalizing my reality. I can do it, or better yet, let Devlin do me. I try convincing myself that it will be quick. Simple. Emotionless. I tilt my head back, looking up at him, and his hand slides up my neck to cup my chin.

The way Devlin looks at me is anything but emotionless.

"I'm taking my time with you, Eve," Devlin says, defying my mind. He bends and presses his lips to mine.

It's the sweetest kiss he's ever given. It's everything I didn't want it to be.

Devlin releases me, standing upright. "It's time for dessert, Eve. Ready my plate," he says.

Little does he know. His plate has been ready since his lips touched mine. I may need to run it through the rinse cycle before he puts anything on it.

"Mind if I freshen up first?"

Devlin smirks knowingly. "Whatever you need. Just don't take too long. Dessert is my favorite part of the meal."

I go to my room to freshen up and regroup. I stay until I feel my mind is in a place where the act won't matter as much as it did before I left.

When I return, Devlin sits at the table with his ankle resting on his knee, bare-chested, wearing only thin layered shorts. I go straight to the bed, flip the cover back, and lie down. I'm ready to get it over with, so I can move on with my life.

Braced on my elbow, I bend my knees and spread my legs, gazing at Devlin expectantly. I feign confidence, behaving like this is one of my assignments for work, and it has to be done.

"Prepped and ready," I told him.

"So, eager," Devlin responds. He stands, retrieves an ice bowl with a covered tray inside from the cart, and stalks toward me.

"And you're talking too much."

Devlin sets the tray on the nightstand and sits facing me on the bed. "Rest your head," he says, and I obey, lying my head on the pillow.

I watch Devlin, waiting, ready for his move. He grabs an ice cube from the bowl and hovers over me. His lips are so close I can hardly stand it. A drop of liquid trails over my breast, stirring my longing.

Devlin claims my mouth as he presses the cube to my nipple. I moan at the stinging pain of the ice and the delight of his lips hitting me all at once. My inhibitions disappear, and I bask in the caress of his tongue, meeting mine.

Devlin kisses my collarbone. His lips tread lightly over my skin until his mouth replaces the cube, clamping over my nipple and sucking.

I clutch my thighs at the abrupt chill to my clit.

Devlin pauses, his hand trapped in my grip, and lifts his eyes to mine. "Open up, Eve. Unless you want me to stop."

I shake my head, releasing my grip. "No. Don't stop," I panted.

The ice remains for seconds longer, numbing the pain away. Numbness turns to a deep throb when Devlin removes the cube. I feel the thrum through my entire body. I want him to take it away and do whatever he needs to cure the ache.

"Devlin," I breathe his name, pleading for him to continue.

"In time, Eve."

"Now," I responded.

Devlin sucks in a sharp breath, his eyes closing for a moment. Then, he grabs a handful of berries, his deliberate gaze falling on me.

"Steady," Devlin says as he positions the tiny blue balls on my belly. "Don't move, or I'll have to start again," He warns.

The thought that I shouldn't move, the simple tease of his fingertip against my skin, and the way his eyes find mine after each placement all have my heart racing. It's a wicked dare because Devlin knows the last thing I want is for him to start over.

I glance down, but all I can make out is what looks like a few letters with a single-lined trail beneath them.

Devlin brings a berry to my lips, and I open my mouth to receive it, chewing slowly, careful not to choke. Then he feeds me a few more, balancing the last one on the tip of his tongue and into my mouth.

Devlin kisses me, and it takes everything in me not to move, not to touch him, and pull him to me. He ends the kiss with a touch of his lips to the corner of my mouth.

"My turn," he says, trailing his eyes over the length of me. He moves to kneel at my feet, spreading my legs wider. His thin shorts do little to hide his thick cock pressing against me nor his thigh muscles flexing my ass as his body hovers over me.

My body shivers inside. The pulse at my core quickens with anticipation.

"What is it?" I asked, glancing at the berries covering me.

Devlin smirks, replying, "I'll tell you once I reach the bottom." Then, he begins, plucking the berries from my chest one by one, the tip of his nose and his lips tantalizing, brushing my skin. He pulls the final berry between his lips, his tongue swirling it inside the dip in my belly before dragging it lower until it disappears.

"What did it say?" I asked again.

Devlin gazes at me with more passion than I've ever seen. He squeezes my thighs, his jaw ticking as he stares at me.

"You tell me," He answers.

Devlin dips his head lower, his warm breath coating me. Then, pulls my clit into his mouth and sucks.

I never knew how good dessert could be at the expense of someone else's mouth. It doesn't take long to realize the answer Devlin wouldn't give. But I know it. I feel it as if it's the only truth I've ever known. It's not the first time his mouth has claimed me, but this time it's a prayer. A promise that regardless of if we're together, I belong to him.

*Mine* is written in every breath, in every sweep of his tongue. It seeps through his fingers and into my veins.

I squirm beneath him, rounding my hips and gripping his head.

Devlin's fingers dig into my thighs, his face bouncing against my pussy as his tongue dives into me.

"I'm," I stutter, pressing my head into the pillow. "Coming." My back arches and starlight bounces against my eyelids as I cry out, "Yours."

My body collapses.

Devlin moans, continuing to lap at me until there's nothing left. He licks his lips when he comes up for air and moves to lie next to me. His eyes are like fire, burning into mine.

"You're beautiful, Eve," he says, sliding his fingers over my forehead. "You're a lot for one man to handle," he says, and I can't decide if it's a compliment, an insult, or both.

Devlin is speaking as if this is goodbye, and we'll never see each other again. I get it. No more screwing around. But does he have to be so dramatic? Dramatics aren't good in this situation.

I don't know how to respond, so I just stare.

Devlin flattens his back to the mattress and opens his arms to me. "Come here," he beckons me over.

I go willingly, snuggling into his side.

We stare at the ceiling. No words, just Devlin rubbing my arm with my ear partial to his chest, my hand resting just below.

"I wish I could go back," Devlin whispers cryptically after a long stretch of silence.

This time, I don't dare ask Devlin what he means. His answers always lead to more questions. Instead, I enjoy the moment that will soon be over.

Our dessert was phenomenal.

I ate. Devlin ate, but I feel like I've been fucked thoroughly, in more ways than one.

How do I move on from this?

# Chapter 24

**Devlin**

LAST NIGHT WHILE Eve slept peacefully in my arms, I realized something. I can't let her go. I want to break all the rules and change them if I can't. She's the difference I need in my life, the one person I can no longer do without. Rash decisions aren't really my thing, but the one I'm about to make seems crucial to my survival. I only hope Eve has some humor left in her for me.

"Do you trust me?" As we return home, I stare at Eve sitting next to me on the plane. I expect a smart reply to barrel out of her mouth at any moment.

Eve stares back at me, her eyes softer than usual. She had the same look this morning when she left my room to pack her bags. I was surprised when she didn't immediately want to flee when she woke up.

Eve breathes easily. "I trust you," she says, throwing me off for a moment.

"Good, because I want you to do something for me."

"What is it?"

"When we land, I want to take you to lunch."

Eve gives me a questioning look, grinning a little. "That doesn't require much trust," she says.

"You'll feel different when we get there, but know that I have a life you know little about."

"Are you back to playing games because my energy is spent, Devlin? I can't do it anymore."

"I told you I'm done with games. From here on out, I'll be straight with you. Every word from my mouth has meaning."

Eve bites her lip, turning her head toward the window and back. "Okay. I'll go along with whatever this is, but if you're screwing with my head, Devlin," She pauses, threatening me with her eyes.

"There's that charm I love so much," I smiled. "By the way, I meant to ask you something."

Eve squints her eyes in warning but asks, "What?"

I lean close so only she can hear me. "Are you a member of the mile-high club?"

Eve's eyes round to saucers, and she swallows hard. Then she clears her throat, rubbing her hands over her lap. "No," She answers simply.

"We still have a few minutes before we land if you need a hurrah after the hurrah," I added suggestively.

Eve scoffs. "Oh, God. Some things never change."

"Hey," I said defensively. "I'm a work in progress. Besides, you'd hate me if I changed everything about myself. There are parts that I'm sure you enjoy."

Eve rolls her eyes and turns toward the window, remaining until the flight lands.

VICTORIA COULDN'T PICK us up at the airport, so Eve and I caught a cab to Breck's Bagels for lunch. Eve looked surprised by my choice when we arrived. I figured it was neutral ground, a place we'd both been.

I ordered a bagel and coffee for each of us. Then, we find a table away from the door and sit across from one another.

Eve wraps her hands around her cup, tapping her finger against it as she looks out the window. "There's nothing like a dose of reality to set things straight. Am I right?" She looks at me, grinning a little.

"What's on your mind, Eve?" I asked sincerely.

"You. Me. Work. The lives we must return to after….,"

"That's actually why we're here."

"Sorry, I'm late. My previous engagement took longer than I thought." Vicky plops down in the chair next to me.

I focus on Eve, noticing a slight shift in her posture. She double blinks at Vicky as if she's confused. Then her eyes land on me. She clears her throat and sips from her cup.

I sent Vicky a text before we boarded the plane, asking her to meet us after her appointment. Eve doesn't look happy about the invite. She tries to hide it behind a blank expression, but I know her. She can't hide from me.

"Am I interrupting something?" Vicky staggers out, looking from me to Eve.

Eve pastes a smile, setting her cup on the table. "No. You're just in time. Devlin was about to tell me why we're here," she says.

Vicky touches Eve's hand on the table. "So, tell me everything. How was the trip? Did you take in any sites? Was Dev on his best behavior?" She fired off questions, ignoring Eve's statement and not giving her a chance to chime in. "I want to know all the details."

I'm sure Vicky would love to hear about what I've been up to with Eve, but it's not happening. Vicky knows where I draw the line about my personal life, and Eve would never disclose the truth.

Eve tries to hold in her blush, but I see straight through her. She's uncomfortable, and every sordid detail of our affair is still fresh on her mind. Her eyes dart to me for help, but I want to know how she'll answer the woman she thinks is my special friend.

"So," Vicky tries again, giving Eve's hand a gentle squeeze.

Eve pulls her hand away from Vicky, joining her fingers together. "There's nothing to tell. It was work. We visited the factory and had dinner with the manager," Eve says, leaving out the parts that mattered most to me. She brings her cup to her lips, peeking over the top.

"Oh," Vicky says, disappointed. "I was hoping you'd tell me Dev was a bad man, that he couldn't keep his hands to himself."

Eve coughs, lowering her cup to the table as her eyes widen.

Vicky laughs. "What? Did I say something wrong? I've been trying to pawn him off for years. He keeps scaring everyone away."

I join in on Vicky's laughter. "I'm not yours to pawn," I told Vicky.

"What is this?" Eve asks angrily, moving her eyes over Vicky and me. "Am I some kind of game to you? A bet to see if I'd fall into your trap? I expect this from Devlin, but I won't sit here and be made a fool of by someone I barely know."

Eve scoots her chair back enough to stand, her eyes squinted to slits. My heart pounds when she turns her back and takes the first step away from me.

I stand quickly and go after Eve. I grab her arm, turning her to face me, and wrapping my arm around her waist, trapping her in my embrace.

"No, Devlin," Eve says, attempting to wiggle free to no avail. "I'm not one of your…."

I pressed my lips to hers before she could finish. She continues to wiggle two seconds longer before she gives in, and her body relaxes. She kisses me back, but it's short-lived.

Eve's eyes fly open, and her head rears back. I think she'll ram her forehead to my nose for a moment, but her feet stomp my toe instead. I ignore the sting, fixating on her.

"What are you doing?" Eve says, her eyes darting to Vicky standing at the table, watching us closely.

I clip her chin, bringing her eyes back to me. "I'm going after what I want. All you have to do is trust me, Eve," I said.

"Is everything alright here, Miss?" A woman with a half apron on asks Eve. She spins a dry cloth through the air, cutting her eyes, daring me to step further out of line.

Eve stares at me for a moment, her jaw set in a hard line, waring with her emotions.

I loosen my hold on her, and she looks at the woman, answering, "Yes. I'm fine. Thanks."

"Glad to assist. I'll be over there if you need anything," The woman tells Eve, staring pointedly at me.

Eve seems uncomfortable with everyone staring at us. I drop my arms, giving her room to breathe.

"We should get out of here. Let's talk in the car," I suggest.

"That's probably a good idea," Eve agreed.

I leave a tip on the table, but it does little to please the woman who offered Eve her assistance. Her eyes don't leave us as we exit the shop with our bags. She likely thinks I'm abusing Eve, but little does she know. I don't have one ill intent for Eve in my body.

We walk to my car silently, and Vicky hands me the keys.

"Aren't you proud of me?" Vicky asks once we're inside the car. "Not one scratch on her," She beams.

"Yeah, thanks for that," I told Vicky while eyeing Eve in the passenger seat.

Vicky insisted Eve sit up front with me against her request. Eve hasn't looked away from me since she sat down. I have a lot of explaining to do. I didn't confirm Vicky's ruse, but I didn't deny it. I was wrong for allowing Eve to believe the worst of me.

Vicky leans forward in the space between our seats. "Someone want to tell me what's going on, or do I have to continue guessing? I didn't imagine that kiss in there. What happened in Mintville?" Her eyes move from one corner to the other.

Eve gives Vicky a regretful look. "I don't know what else to say except I'm sorry," she says.

"Sorry for what?" Vicky asks.

"Look, Eve. There's nothing to apologize for. You didn't do anything wrong. I did. I should've clarified things the first time you met Vicky, but curiosity got the best of me. We had just…." I paused, glancing at Vicky's eager eyes and perked ears, not wanting to reveal too much. "Then, I saw you here with your bag and two cups. It was unfair of me to expect anything from you when I didn't know what I wanted for myself."

"What's the point of all this, Devlin?" Eve asks.

"I feel something for you, Eve, now, then, even before. I'm saying I've found my match."

Eve looks confused. "What about Victoria?" She asks as if Vicky isn't present.

"I never lied about Vicky. She *is* special to me, and she's not going anywhere because she's my sister."

Eve sucks in a breath. "Your sister," she says, unbelieving.

"Now that that's cleared up, Sis, excuse me," Vicky says, cutting between us to turn the air up. She sits back down, pinching the collar of her shirt and fanning with her other hand.

Eve and I watch her until she settles.

"Don't stop on my account. Things were just starting to heat up. All that's missing is the popcorn and Icee. And M&Ms. Can't forget those," Vicky says.

Eve tries and fails to contain her laughter. It's infectious, and I join in with her.

Eve sobers, finding my eyes. "I can't believe I referred to your sister as a booty call." She palms her face for a few seconds before looking at me again.

"Well, I kind of had that one coming. It wasn't all Dev's fault. I played a part too."

"Yes, you did," Eve agrees, her expression now serious.

"I had never seen Dev look at anyone the way he looked at you. Come to think of it, I've never seen him look at anyone else, period. My brother is stingy with his personal life," Vicky says.

"And rightfully so," I said.

"I know. It's none of my business, but look how far I've gotten you." Vicky nodded to Eve.

"Okay. It's time to return you to school," I said, backing out of the park and pulling away.

I think about how right Vicky is. Her presence played a part in my progress with Eve. Whether that progress grows from here is a mystery.

I drop Vicky off at her dorm. Then, I take Eve home. I stopped in her driveway and put the car in park.

"Can we talk about what I said, Eve?" I angled my body toward her, and she did the same to me.

"I appreciate you telling me about Victoria, and I heard everything else you said, but it changes nothing. Our feelings may have been skewed momentarily, but our status hasn't changed. The rules won't change," Eve says.

"What if they did? We can write our own rules, Eve." I tangle my hands in hers over the console.

Eve stares at our hands for a moment, tightening and loosening her fingers with mine. "We're not these people, Devlin. Rules weren't made to be broken. They were made to be followed."

"Then, those rules weren't made for us."

Eve swallows, her eyes kissing mine once again. Her conflicting emotions swirl into me like a tangible thing, ripping me apart and putting me back together again.

"Eve," I continued, lifting my hand to her cheek. "There's nothing or no one more captivating than you. You infuriate me, and I've tried to ignore it, to give you the space you asked for, but I can't. I won't give you up. Not ever."

"You have to," Eve says. "Even if things were different, I want more than what you can give. You can't just flip a switch and be someone else."

"I'm not trying to be someone else. I want to be a better me. The man you deserve."

"And you honestly think you can be that man?"

"We'll never know unless you agree to try."

"I don't know, Devlin. It could get messy," Eve says.

I watch her, reading through her intricate lines. She's worried about her job if we don't work out. She's terrified that maybe we will. I'm confident that nothing in this world would be more fitting than Eve and me. She's the only woman I'll ever allow the chance to break me. The only woman I'm willing to risk my heart for.

"You said you've never been in love." I slide my thumb over her cheek. "Well, I'm asking you to try. Fall in love with me, Eve."

# Chapter 25

**Evelyn**

I'M SPEECHLESS.

Fall in love with Devlin.

What would that even be like?

I never expected those words to fall from Devlin's mouth, so I didn't know how to respond as I stared at him. He already owns my body. Now he's asking for my heart too. There's so much at stake, so much for me to lose. But as I gaze into his eyes, I know I'll regret it if I don't try.

"I can't promise love, Devlin."

"It would be weird if you could," Devlin chuckles nervously, showing a side of himself I don't see often. "I'm just asking for a chance. Let me woo you, Eve."

Devlin. Vulnerable. An olive branch that decided for me.

"When you put it like that, how can I say no?" I smile, just as nervous as I commit to the unknown. "How do we do this, Devlin? What about work?"

Devlin leans closer, keeping his hand on the side of my face. "Let me worry about that."

"I'm sorry, but I can't just put my whole life in your hands on a whim," I said calmly. "I think we should keep this arrangement to ourselves, at least until we know where it's going."

Devlin smiles, appearing amused. "You want me to be your dirty little secret."

"And I'll be yours," I said. "It's the only way we stand a chance."

"I like the sound of that."

"What?"

"We." Devlin traces the outline of my mouth with his thumb. "Should we seal it with a kiss?" He moves even closer until his breath skims my lips.

I lift a finger, pressing it to his mouth. "I don't kiss on the lips," I teased. I turn away from him, attempting to exit the car, when he grabs my arm, pulling me back to him. I yelped at the sudden movement.

Devlin's breath crosses my lips again as his eyes bore into mine. "Neither did I, but things change," he says. He kisses me fervidly, and I lean into it, kissing him back.

I pull away after a few seconds, needing to catch my breath. My heart thumps carelessly as I pry my eyes open to look at Devlin as if it senses trouble on the horizon.

"I feel it too, Eve," Devlin says.

"Feel what?"

"The spark just got a little bit stronger."

"I need to go," I said, hating that he's right because what if it does work out? What if our spark grows so strong we can't contain it, and it fizzles just as fast? "See you tomorrow." I pull away from Devlin, and he lets me go this time.

"Tomorrow," I heard Devlin's voice slip through the crack in the door before it closed.

I can feel Devlin watching me as I walk hastily toward my house. Something about his eyes at my back feels different now. His bad intentions turned good, and the shift is noticeably enticing.

I close the door behind me once inside, flattening my back against it. I wait for the soft purr of Devlin's engine to evaporate. Then, I take a deep breath, fanning my hand in front of my face.

I must have left half my brain in Mintille because why else would I agree to Devlin's proposal? The fear of regret made me do it. Now I have to live with my decision. Recanting is not an option. With Devlin, once an offer is accepted, he'll stop at nothing to close the deal.

I pace the floor in my living room for a few seconds before collapsing on the couch. Staring up at the ceiling, I decide it's time to call my sanity. Holland is the only one I trust to talk me through this because there is no way I'm getting out. I'm in too deep.

I STRIDE INTO WORK the next morning, feeling the most anxious I've ever felt.

Talking to Holland over the phone last night calmed me. And in Holland fashion, he told me to dive in and give it a chance. He said I wouldn't have agreed if it wasn't already in my mind. Everything he said made sense, but the wildcard I'm bound to run into at any moment today is no match for sensibility.

My faux confidence guides me to my office, ignoring the eyes I think are bearing down on me. I leave the door open and sit behind my desk, relieved there wasn't a Devlin sighting on the way in. As I stare across the shared space, I'm grateful for the empty office across from me.

I settled into work, pouring over a new submission I'd received last week.

The day flows easily, and I'm kind of disappointed when lunchtime approaches and Devlin is still nowhere to be found. I begin to think that I'd imagined everything since we left Breck's.

I'm focused on the papers on my desk when I hear my door close.

I look up, trying to remain unphased, as Devlin walks toward me. "It's moving day," he says.

"Moving day?" I questioned, knowing full well what he meant.

"Yes. You next to me. Remember?"

Oh, I remember. I was hoping he would forget. I'm not sure it's safe for us to be so close.

"What's the expected time?" I asked.

"Maintenance will be here around two." Devlin rounds my desk, stopping beside me. He bends his body, taking my mouse in his hands, with his eyes on my screen as he whispers in my ear. "But there's something I've always wanted to do here," he says.

"What's that?"

"Have lunch in your office."

Before I can protest, Devlin pulls my chair back and drops to his knees, disappearing beneath my desk. He pulls me to the edge and widens my legs, dipping his head between them.

My eyes flash up, noticing the unlocked door.

"Devlin, you can't," I breathe, making no move to stop him.

"Tell me to stop, and I will," he says, peeking up at me.

But I don't. The words don't come. My limbs don't move.

Cool air hits my core as he slides my panties to one side, replaced by the warmth of his breath.

I should get up and tell him to stop, but I can't. I want his mouth on me. I welcome the risk.

"Talk to me, Eve. Tell me about your morning." Devlin's odd request reaches my mind just as his tongue makes contact.

I grip the arms of my chair, sucking in a deep breath, trying to focus on the question while enjoying the feel of him lapping the course between my lips.

"I, I…. It was uneventful. Nothing out of the norm except your absence," I told him.

"Mmm," Devlin hums.

"I've been occupied with the new submission. Barely had time to…." I gasped. "Breathe."

"And how's your breathing now?" Devlin asks, dipping his tongue deep inside and circling his thumb over me. He pulls my clit between his lips, pressing hard.

I gulp, kicking out uncontrollably, my feet hitting the underside of the desk with a loud thud.

Seconds later, a knock sounds, and I jump, eyeing the door.

"Evelyn. It's Susan." Her muffled voice seems to pierce my ear.

I'm frozen in place, caught in the act. The one time I did something daring in the office was the one time Susan decided to visit me. What could she possibly want with me?

"Tell her to come in," Devlin says, breaking through my frenzied thoughts.

"But...."

"Invite her in." Devlin kisses my inner thigh, ignoring my concern.

His command excites me more than the threat of being found out. Against my better judgment, I said, "Come in."

"What can I do for you?" I asked Susan when she stepped inside.

"Is everything alright in here," Susan asks, looking around my office. "I thought I heard a loud noise."

Devlin continues to lap at my core, his fingers diving inside over and over again.

"Oh, that," I said, pursing my lips for a moment. I slide the chair forward a fraction, pressing my palms to the desk, and smiling at Susan. "Everything's fine. I got a little excited and kicked the desk," I said truthfully. My leg flexed again as Devlin sucked, and my foot lashed at the desk once more. "See."

"Hmm. It echoed pretty loudly," Susan sighs. "Well, I'll get out of your hair," she says, turning to leave, then stopping and turning back. "Have you seen Devlin? I guess I'm supposed to report to him in Mr. Sawyer's absence. An adjustment for sure," she says.

Devlin flicks his tongue over me, gripping my thighs, and I stifle a moan.

"I uh," I paused, clearing my throat. "I think he's at lunch." I feel Devlin's quiet chuckle below.

"Jan and I were about to run out too. Would you like anything?" Susan asks.

My smile widens.

*I would like for you to leave.*

"No, thanks," I answered.

"By the way, I heard you are moving today," Susan says.

"Yes," I said shortly, hoping she'll get the hint and leave.

Susan pauses, looking around my office again. "Well, let me know if you need help."

"Thanks, Susan."

Susan leaves, closing the door behind her.

I close my eyes and release a long breath.

"Your acting skills and control are phenomenal, Eve," Devlin says, drawing my attention to him. "But I need you to go off script now. I want you to come for me," he says, sliding his fingers over me and dropping his head into position again.

Instead of pushing Devlin away as I should, I relax, letting him devour me. He parts my lips with his fingers, burying his face between my thighs. Within seconds, I let go, suppressing my moan, leaning against the chair and gripping his head as I erupt into his mouth.

When my head stops spinning, I slide my chair back.

Devlin rises to his feet, pulls two tissues from the box on my desk, and wipes his mouth. He kisses my lips briefly, then rounds the desk to leave.

"This is going to be fun," Devlin says, stopping once he reaches the door to look at me. "You're effing beautiful, Eve."

"Effing?" I question, biting my bottom lip.

"Effing beautiful," Devlin repeats. "Gotta keep it clean in the office, Eve." He winks. Then he's gone.

I can't help but grin at his reasoning. What we did was not cleanliness in the office. It was wild, daring, and dangerous. But he's right. It was fun.

# Chapter 26

**Devlin**

IT'S NEARLY FIVE o'clock when I pause beneath the frame of Eve's new office. I still can't believe she agreed to try with me. I watch her for a few seconds arranging supplies on her desk before walking up behind her, leaving only inches of space.

Eve startles at my proximity, looking over her shoulder. "What are you doing?" She asks.

"Welcoming you to the neighborhood." I drag her hair over her shoulder, my fingers brushing her skin along the way, then stuff my hands into my pockets.

"Devlin," Eve sighs. "We had an agreement, and you're dangerously close." She turns to face me. "Someone might see."

"I know," I said, stepping forward a fraction. "I have a hard time keeping my distance."

Eve smiles, stepping back, her thighs meeting the desk. "You'll have to try harder."

"Go out with me tonight," I suggest.

"Out, out?"

"Dinner at my place unless you're ready to showcase us to the world."

"Your place it is."

"I'll pick you up at seven." I watch Eve for a while, wishing I could touch her before I go. But I honor her wishes and keep my distance.

"MAKE YOURSELF AT home," I told Eve when we entered my home.

"Are you sure because there's a lot I didn't see the last time I was here?"

"Feel free to look around. There's not much to see. A couple more bedrooms and empty walls. I'm a clean slate ready to be filled."

Our eyes meet, and Eve clears her throat, looking away.

"What's for dinner?" She asks.

"Pasta with baked salmon. I hope that's okay." I know the parts of Eve she wanted me to see, but there are things I don't know about her that I wish to learn.

"Sounds good."

Eve took me up on my offer to look around while I prepared dinner. I'm not afraid in the least that she'll find something incriminating. I don't want to hold back from her anymore.

As we sit at the table eating our meal, I realize how much I enjoy having Eve share my space. It's good to have her back. I hope she's the missing key, the woman I'm meant to spend my life with.

"So, your friend, Holland." I watch Eve across the table.

"What about him?" Eve asks.

"I take it you told him about us, our new relationship."

"I did."

"Then he approves," I conclude.

"What makes you say that?"

I smile. "If he didn't, we wouldn't be here. You obviously value his friendship. I think it's good you have that."

Eve tilts her head to the side. "And you don't feel threatened by Holland?"

"I don't," I answered confidently. "If you wanted Holland, you wouldn't be here with me, and he would never allow it if he felt the same." I pause, considering telling her the whole truth. If we are going to work, she has to know. "But that's not entirely true when it comes to anyone else. I'm a greedy man, Eve, cautious of anyone who occupies your time."

"Sounds controlling to me," Eve says, centering her head and furrowing her brows.

"I could never control you. I wouldn't dare to try. Unless we're in the bedroom."

Eve blushes. "Good thing because that wouldn't bode well for you," she says.

I chuckle, dragging a napkin over my lips. I finish my drink and stand, offering Eve my hand. I guide her to the living room and put on some slow tunes. Then I pull her into my arms as close as our bodies allow.

"You're a dancer, huh?" Eve says, gazing into my eyes.

"You're bringing out the best in me," I said as we swayed to the music. "I'm a lover and a dancer. I'm going all in, Eve, and I'm not coming out without a fight."

Eve looks away, lying her head on my chest. "Is Victoria your only sibling?" She asks suddenly.

I keep the tempo with the music while gathering my thoughts. I knew I'd have to discuss my family at some point. That's what relationships are about, getting to know more about each other.

"She is." *For now.*

"And your parents?"

"My mother and father were never together. My mother passed away years ago, and my father married Shana, Vicky's mom."

"Sorry about your mom," Eve says.

"No need to be sorry. It's been years. I'm okay with it now."

"You don't talk much about your dad."

"My father can be a hard man to cope with. He's a conversation for another day," I said, not wanting to ruin the evening. My father is a subject I'll have to ease Eve into. I can't just spring it on her because she may not understand. "Do you mind if we change the subject?"

"Sure. What do you want to talk about?"

"Do you have a family other than Holland?"

"My parents are both well. They moved three states away after my graduation. We talk occasionally, but I barely get a chance to see them. The same goes for my older sister. She went away to college and never came back. I'm the one who got stuck," Eve grins.

"Maybe we can see them together one day," I propose.

"Maybe."

"I'm glad you got stuck, Eve," I whispered.

"Wow, you're a ball of motivation," Eve grins.

"I just mean that I'm glad you're still here, that you didn't move away. Or we might not have met," I explained. Eve seems to settle onto me even more. We dance silently through the next song with her arms wrapped around my neck and my arms around her waist.

When the song ends, Eve looks at me inquisitively. "Am I safe with you, Devlin?" She asks.

I stare back at her with my heart and mind open to give and receive. Tucking her hair behind her ear, I answered, "There's no safer place."

"You're safe with me too," Eve says.

I press my lips to her forehead, letting her words sink in, feeling them to my core. "Spend the night with me."

Eve lifts her eyes to mine. She hesitates, opening and closing her mouth. Her hands fall to the side of my arms, and her eyes blink at my chin.

I cup my hands around her face, guiding her eyes back to me. "I'm not ready to let you go."

Eve swallows. "I don't want you to," She admits.

I brush my thumb over her cheek, dropping my other hand to her arm.

"My bedroom is down the hall, second door on the right. We can share, or you can take one of the others. The choice is yours. I just want you here." I gently kiss her lips, release her, and go to my room.

I leave my room door open while I get comfortable, stripping down to my boxers. I pull the comforter back and sit on the edge of the bed, listening, waiting to see what Eve decides.

Three minutes pass before she appears inside the door frame, and relief fills me.

Eve walks toward me, blushing, but refusing to look away. She stops in front of my dresser and clears her throat. "Do you have a shirt I can borrow?" She asks.

I nod, walk to where she stands, and open the second drawer on her left. I retrieve a white T-shirt and sit it on the dresser.

"Do you mind?" I asked Eve as I tugged at the tale of her shirt.

She lifts her arms in response, and I pull the shirt over her head, placing it neatly on the dresser. I unbutton her jeans, sliding them over her hips, down to her feet, and she steps out.

My eyes pour over her body, noticing every curve, every hard and soft line, the perfect and imperfect. Silently declaring her mine.

"Did you wear this for me?" I ask of her midnight lingerie.

"No. I wore it for me. You just get to reap the benefits," Eve answers.

"Well, I love your benefits," I said, tracing the curve of her bra with my finger. I tilt my head, retracing the lines with my lips, delicately kissing her breast.

Eve's breathing picks up as her fingers squeeze the dresser's edge. When my tongue dips between her breast, she pulls my head up and presses her lips to mine, kissing me fervently.

I kiss her back, gripping her thighs, lifting her, and spreading her legs around my waist. I place her on the dresser's edge and step back, tugging her panties down as she lifts her ass. I grab a condom from the top drawer and step out of my boxers. Eve watches with bated breath as I rip the packet with my teeth, remove the condom, and slide it on.

I slip two fingers into my mouth, wetting them. Then, I pump my cock as I slide one finger inside Eve, then another. She gasps, her hands sprinting to my shoulders.

"Eve," I said, thinking of all the things I want to do to her, all the ways I want to have her. The time I want to spend buried deep inside her.

"It's yours," she says as if reading my mind.

I remove my fingers, my dick replacing them, slowly curving into Eve. I breathe deeply when I reach the hilt, soaking in the feel of her finally wrapped around me again. I have to make it last. I don't want it to end.

Eve's fingers dig into my shoulders as I move steadily inside her. She moans softly, loudly, and soft again, her hips one with the tide, our bodies akin to the wave. She's too good. Too tight. Too wet. Too much of everything.

*I want this to last.*

I lift Eve from the dresser, dropping her feet to the floor, and pull out of her completely, thinking a change in position might help. I twist her body toward the mirror, tilting her forward. She seems confused and irritated at first but settles when I squeeze her cheeks and give her a tender smack on her ass.

A taunting smile graces Eve's lips. I tease her breast and pinch her nipple between my fingers. Then I test the waters again, diving back inside her.

I grip her hips, watching her reaction in the mirror as I pound into her. And within seconds, I knew I'd made a mistake. This position feels even better than the last. The buildup comes quick, and I know I won't be able to stop it.

Eve whips her hips against me, her breast bouncing out of her bra as she watches me.

"Fuck, Eve," I groan. "What have you done to me? I can't hold it," I admit.

Eve bites her bottom lip as she continues to grind against me. Then she throws my words back at me. "Come for me, Devlin."

I erupt at Eve's words. My fingers dig into her hips as my body stiffens, holding her flush against me. My eyes closed, and I grunted loudly as I came.

I ease out, releasing Eve from my grip. When she turns to face me, I kiss her.

"You amaze me, Eve."

"It's all about the benefits," she says.

I chuckle softly. "What am I gonna do with you?" I asked, touching my forehead to hers.

"I imagine all sorts of things," Eve says, pecking my lips and slinking out of my arms.

I follow her into the bathroom, and we take a shower together. Then, I slide my oversized shirt onto her, and we go to bed.

Eve falls asleep in my arms, and I follow shortly after, thinking *I could get used to this.*

# Chapter 27

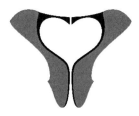

*Three Months Later*

**Evelyn**

I DIDN'T THINK I would end up with Devlin, of all people. But *we* work, and when he woos, he woos. There's so much more to him than people think. He's still the same flirty, annoying man but also sweet, kind, and caring.

I couldn't stop myself from falling for Devlin once I started. I've spent more time at his place than mine in the past month because his requests are hard to refuse. I'd like to say everything is perfect, but I don't want to jinx us.

We've done well keeping our relationship a secret for the past three months. At least, I think we have. No one has said anything. Though, I think Susan may suspect something. She's been giving me the same stink eye she's always given Devlin lately. It's exciting, having this secret that no one knows but us, but I want more. I know secrecy was my idea, but I want to be known as the woman who captured Devlin's heart. Though, I wonder if the thrill will dissipate once everyone finds out.

"Evelyn."

I jumped in my chair, looking toward the sound of Devlin's voice entering my office, smiling at the man I'd grown to know so well. He strides toward me with purpose, and a small smile curves his lips. Only hours ago, I was in his bed with his arms covering me. The back of my neck still tingles from the tender caress of his lips teasing my skin.

"Must be important. You never call me that," I said.

"Today's a special day," he says.

"How can I forget." I stand, then walk around my desk to stand in front of him two feet away. I rest my hands on the edge of the desk to avoid touching him. "Today is the official day you take my job," I teased.

It was a pipe dream to believe I could be in his position. I honestly thought it would be Charity, but I was wrong. It's become a running joke with Devlin and me now.

Charity came back to work last week, and even she seemed surprised by the turn of events. I'm curious how she feels with today being Mr. Sawyer's last day in the office. The two of them seemed so familiar before she got hurt.

"I can't take something you never had," Devlin quips playfully.

Intimate silence fills the space between us, our eyes locked in place.

Devlin removes a foot of space and stops. "You're effing sexy, Eve. It's taking everything not to bend you over that desk," he says.

"I'm all yours," I said. Devlin lifts a hand to my cheek, and I swat it away. "But, not right now," I grin. "What did you want to see me about?"

"I want to see you about everything, Eve." Devlin licks his lips, tucking his hands into his pockets.

"Can you, at least, try to be serious for more than a minute."

"I was serious all morning. Then I saw you."

I glance at the desk, considering taking him up on his offer. Then, I shake the thought from my head. "Mr. Sawyer is in the building," I remind him.

"Right," Devlin drags out. "I knew there was another reason I stopped by. I need an escort to my celebratory luncheon slash Sawyer sendoff."

"You think us showing up together is a good idea?" I asked.

Devlin shrugs. "It's not a bad idea. We're colleagues. It's perfectly normal to be in the same office, walk the halls, even ride the elevator together," he says, twitching his brows.

"Devlin," I warned.

He laughs. "Okay. No funny business. I promise. Even though we can't walk hand in hand, I still want to share the moment with you."

"When you put it that way," I pause, glancing around him, then kiss his lips quickly. "Let's go," I said, walking around him toward the door.

Devlin follows my lead to the elevator, and we step inside. He keeps his hands in his pockets, cutting his eyes at me. I press the button for the first floor and look forward.

"You kissed me," Devlin says.

I give him a coy smile. "I did."

"I have the urge to return the favor right now," He smirks.

"You wouldn't," I scoffed.

"I love a good dare," Devlin says, pulling his hand out of his pocket and wrapping his arm around my waist. He pulls me to him and presses his lips to mine, kissing me softly. He releases me, returning to his position as if nothing happened. The elevator halts, doors open, and he looks at me. "After you," he says.

Heat fills my cheeks as I stare at him, unbelieving. I want to lash out at Devlin, cause a scene, tell him how unfair he was, but that wouldn't be good for either of us. Instead, I smile, my eyes promising revenge.

I exit the elevator silently with Devlin at my back. I can practically feel his smug smile burning a hole through me as we step into the lobby.

The lobby is full of employees standing around holding semi-private conversations. A few heads turn in our direction, and I blush, feeling like they know what happened in the elevator. Rectangular tables line the wall opposite the elevator, topped with punch and finger foods. A sheet cake is centered amongst the other items.

Mr. Sawyer critically eyes Devlin from the table's end before honing in on me. He holds my gaze, throwing me off center. It's unnerving and unwanted, but I can't look away. I don't think the man has a soft spot anywhere in his anatomy. It's probably best that Devlin got the position and not me. Mr. Sawyer is far too intense for my liking.

Claps and cheer ring out, cutting my brief connection with Mr. Sawyer. Being in the spotlight with Devlin is even more unsettling.

I walk toward the table, leaving Devlin to bask in his glory. I don't look back to see his reaction because I may just melt. His kiss still tingles my lips, so I don't risk it.

I pour myself a drink and take a few sips, turning when I hear Mr. Sawyer's voice above the chatter.

"Quiet down a moment, everyone," Mr. Sawyer says, pausing until it's silent. "As most of you know, I'm stepping back from day-to-day operations. Devlin Hughs has adopted that role."

Mr. Sawyer continues talking, but it's background noise in my ear when I look at Devlin. He's standing next to Mr. Sawyer now with his hands in his pockets, soaking up everyone's attention. He wore my favorite suit today—a two-piece, black-on-black with a matching shirt and a red tie. I still can't believe he's mine.

As if Devlin can sense my thoughts, he looks at me, sending a smile my way. I quickly revert my eyes before anyone notices.

Someone across the room shouts, *"speech,"* after Mr. Sawyer finishes speaking. Devlin says a few words, his eyes giving and sincere as they move over the crowd. My co-workers give him the same respect as they had Mr. Sawyer, and I couldn't be more proud of the man he is.

Heather, the receptionist, appears next to me at the table once Devlin's done talking. She grabs a plate and two-quarter sandwiches.

"So, are you like Mr. Hughes' assistant now?" Heather asks.

My eyes snapped to her, hoping she didn't mean it as an insult. I never know with my co-workers. Their filters are very thin.

"No. I have the same job I've always had. I just moved to the other side of the building," I answered.

Heather turns with the plate in her hand. "Do you know if he needs one?" She asks.

I follow Heather's eyes to Devlin, then look back at her. "No," I said confidently.

"Hmm. Maybe I'll ask him," Heather says, disregarding my answer.

"Maybe you should," I said. I'd like to see how far Heather gets and the look on her face when Devlin turns her down.

I face the table—through with Heather—and fix myself a bowl of fruit. Then, I go back to my office alone.

Ten minutes later, Devlin walks in with a piece of cake and sits it in front of me.

"This D is for you," Devlin says, wiggling his brows.

I can't help but laugh at his corny joke as I glance at the cake with DEV drawn across it in huge letters.

"Why'd you leave?" Devlin asks.

"Why did you leave?" I returned his question. "It's your party."

"I don't care about the party. I care about you. Now, tell me what's bothering you," Devlin says, sitting on the edge of my desk. "You bolted like a fire was under you."

"Talking to Heather got me thinking."

"What did she say?"

I clear my throat, slightly ashamed of my bout of jealousy. Devlin hasn't given me a reason to think he would cheat.

"She wants to be your *assistant*," I said.

Devlin laughs, but I don't see the humor.

"Oh, you think it's funny?"

"Yes," Devlin says, then sobers. "But I also think it's effing sexy how much you care." He clips my chin, then releases it, returning his hand to his lap.

A throat clears, and Devlin and I turn toward it.

Mr. Sawyer's arms hang tense at his side as he stares at us. I've never seen him angry until now.

"Evelyn," Mr. Sawyer addresses me. Then his eyes move to Devlin. "I'd like to see you in my office before I go," he tells Devlin.

Mr. Sawyer disappears, and Devlin takes his sweet time standing, undaunted.

"You have nothing to worry about," Devlin says, but I'm unsure. I fear our arrangement has come to an end.

Devlin walks around the desk and presses his lips to my temple. I don't pull away because it may just be the last.

"Don't worry," he says.

My eyes follow him out the door, along with my hope that we will last.

# Chapter 28

**Devlin**

"CLOSE THE DOOR," Sawyer says as I walk inside his office.

I do as he says, then step further inside. I knew this conversation was bound to happen at some point, so I'm ready for it. I know what he will say and what I'm going to do.

Sawyer comes around his desk and paces in front of it. He stops before me, pinching the bridge of his nose, and shaking his head. His eyes are cold when he looks at me, but

I'm not afraid. We have a difference of opinion that we'll sort out soon enough.

"What are you thinking?" Sawyer's voice booms. "That was not platonic. I warned you not to go down that road," he says. "This fling or whatever it is between you and Evelyn must stop," he demands.

"I understand. I've got it handled," I answered calmly.

"Do you? Because your actions in there were out of line. If you keep moving in that direction, I'll have no choice but to let one of you go."

Sawyer's words raised a red flag, and I snapped to attention. "Eve is not going anywhere," I told him. "I'd quit before I let you fire her." I know I'm out of line. He's still the owner. I still work for him, but the thought of Eve losing her job because of me is unacceptable.

Sawyer narrows his eyes, warning me to proceed with caution.

"I apologize for my tone, but I'm asking you not to do anything rash. I'll handle it. I promise."

"You'd better. You have until Monday to fix this mess you've made, or I'll do it for you," Sawyer warns.

"Monday. Got it, Boss."

"Hmm," Sawyer grunts returning to his chair. "Dismissed," he says.

I leave Sawyer and go to my office next door.

I have the weekend to decide the course of my future and what I'll do next because I meant it. Eve isn't going anywhere unless she desires.

SHANA HAD THE BABY last month, so dad summoned Vicky and me to Sunday dinner to meet our baby brother. It's the first time I wasn't terribly annoyed with the invite. I can't wait to meet the little guy. I hope he looks like his mom and doesn't have dad's permanent scowl.

"Are you sure it's okay that I came with you?" Eve wonders from the passenger seat of my car.

Sawyer expects me to end things with Eve, but I can't let her go. When I got the call for family dinner, I couldn't think of anyone better to have at my father's table than Eve. I've gotten so deep in the ocean that it's too late to try and float away. She's a part of my family now.

I parked the car in Dad's driveway, staring at the house. I've already broken so many rules. Why not add another one? What's one more angry person on the list?

"Yeah. It's fine. My family will love you. Come on," I answered Eve.

We exit the car, and Eve's questioning gaze walks me to the door. I ring the doorbell, offering her a reassuring smile.

"Do they at least know someone is coming with you?" Eve asks.

"No."

"Not cool, Devlin," Eve says, frustrated.

The door swings open, and Vicky answers, her eyes moving from me to Eve. Her shocked expression morphs into one of amusement.

"Evelyn. Dev," Vicky greets. "And here I thought family dinner would be a bust. I love the two of you together. Always entertaining. Come on in."

Vicky moves aside for Eve and me to enter. We follow her into the living room and sit.

"Mom is in diaper changing mode, but dinner is done. Dad hasn't made his debut yet," Vicky says.

"Debut?" Eve questions.

Vicky beams at Eve. "Oh, this is going to be interesting. You'll see." Vicky looks at me. "I see you still haven't mastered the ways of women yet, Dev."

"Maybe we should help set the table." I changed the subject.

"It's done," Vicky says. "But we can go in. Mom should be down any minute now. Or, since you're in a rebellious mood, you could be the one to make an entrance this time," Vicky suggests.

I smile, considering the idea. It's bad enough that I brought Eve along. Arriving late to the dinner table would certainly grind Dad's gears. I don't want to press my luck.

"Let's grab a seat at the table," I told them.

As we exit the living room, Shana descends the stairs with Brian cuddled in her arms.

"Devlin, you made it," Shana says excitedly. Motherhood agrees with her. She appears sleep deprived but still pretty. Her eyes move to Eve standing next to me. "And you brought a guest," she says nervously.

"Shana, this is Evelyn, my better half." It feels weird saying it out loud. I've never introduced us as a couple before due to the secrecy of our relationship, but this is my family. I should be able to tell them the truth, regardless of the consequences.

"Nice to meet you, Evelyn. Aren't you a nice surprise?" Shana's smile remains as she looks at me. "Mitchell will be beside himself," She adds lightly, but I hear the warning in her voice.

"Do you mind if I hold him?" I asked, nodding to Brian in Shana's arms. Maybe Dad's reaction won't be so bad with the baby around.

"Not at all," Shana replies, happily placing Brian in my arms.

The ladies walk past me into the dining room, and we sit. Eve is next to me, Vicky across from us, and Shana at one end of the table.

"Here." Shana passes me a bottle of milk. "He just woke up, and he's dry. Hunger usually follows," she says, her eyes sparkling as she stares at Brian.

"Thanks," I said, looking down at Brian. His resemblance to Shana and Vicky is uncanny, as I had hoped. He squirms in my arms, poking his bottom lip as his face frowns. I tease the nipple of the bottle to his mouth, and he opens it, his tiny fist clamping around the bottle, practically pushing it inside.

I smile at Brian, thinking of my future. The idea of having children is neither appealing nor unappealing. If it's in the cards for me, it will happen. But Brian is adorable, and I wouldn't mind spending more time with him, teaching him the ways of men. Though, my father likely wouldn't allow it.

I glance at Eve, watching me closely with an unusually pleasing look on her face. "What?" I asked her.

"You're a natural," Eve says, nodding to Brian.

"I don't know about that. This little guy is making it look easy. Aren't you Brian?" I asked quietly in my baby voice.

"Fever," Vicky says over a cough.

I chuckle, and Eve joins in. We've never discussed having babies before, but I can picture it—Eve and me with a kid, maybe more.

"One step at a time, Vicky," I said.

My ears perk at the faint footsteps getting closer, and I fix my eyes on the doorway. Tenacity takes hold of me as Dad comes into view. He stops just past the awning, his eyes skirting around the table and stopping at Eve. Then his nose flares as he looks at me.

I hear Eve's sharp intake of breath next to me, but my eyes remain on Dad. He takes slow, deep breaths as he continues to the table and sits.

"What's the meaning of this, Devlin?" Dad asks, too calmly, and I silently thank Brian for his mild reaction.

"The meaning of what?" I asked as if I didn't already know.

"You, bringing *her* to dinner."

"It's simple. You told me to fix my mess. Well, this is me handling it."

Vicky snorts.

Dad's eyes flit to her in warning, then back to me.

"You know damn well what I meant, Son." Dad narrows his eyes at me.

*Son.*

He only calls me son when I step out of line and need to remember my place. "I'm aware of who I am, *Dad*, but my life is my own. You're not in control of...."

"Silence," Dad hisses.

Out of the corner of my eye, I see Eve's head jerk back at Dad's command.

Shana stands and walks over to me, reaching for Brian. "I'm gonna take him and let you all talk," she says, cupping Brian in her arms and vacating the room.

Dad continues after Shana leaves, his voice more prominent. "You are my son, the head of my company. I won't have you engaged in unfair practices because it feels right in the now. You are better than that. I won't allow it," Dad says.

"You won't allow it?" I chuckle. "You don't get to decide," I told him.

Dad's back stretched taller. "I may not decide whom you copulate with, but...." His gaze moves to Eve. "Evelyn...."

"Don't speak to her," I cut in. "This is between you and me. Eve is not some flavor of the month. She's not someone I tried and threw away after I got my fill." I swallowed the words, thinking of my mother and him. "Eve means more to me than the job you hold over our heads. I love her. And if you knew me, if *you* loved me, you would know that, and you wouldn't try to take it away."

I can feel the shocked stares of Eve and Vicky over my confession. I never told Eve I loved her, never said the words out loud until now. I don't regret saying them. I only wish Dad hadn't dragged it out of me before I got to tell her first.

I close my eyes and drag a hand over my face. Everything hit me all at once. I shouldn't have bombarded Eve this way, but I couldn't resist defying my father.

The doorbell rings, capturing all our attention.

"Whew," Vicky blows out a breath. "I'll get the door."

Eve glares at me as Vicky walks away. Then she looks at Dad.

"Mr. Sawyer, I apologize for showing up here. I had no idea that he…. That you…." Eve pauses, shaking her head. "If I had known, I never would have come," she says.

"Do you love him?" Dad asks Eve.

"What?" She returns, confused.

"Do you love my son?" He asks.

Eve looks at me, then swallows, her eyes still full of anger, but I see through it—the softness behind her hard gaze, the way her eyes kiss mine even now.

"I…. I do. Love him," She answers.

Dad pinches the bridge of his nose, deep in thought.

We sit quietly in the thick uncertain air until Vicky returns.

"This is becoming one big office party," Vicky jokes.

"Charity, glad you could make it. Please, sit," Dad offers her the seat next to Vicky.

Shana reemerged sans Brian and returned to her seat at the table. "Welcome to our home, Charity."

It's obvious that Vicky, Eve, and I are not in the loop. I remain quiet, waiting to be let in because I've already caused a big enough rift tonight. I can't fathom why Charity would be here unless Dad saw my rebellion coming, and she's his backup plan.

"Are you going to tell them, or should I?" Shana asks Dad.

My eyes move from Shana to Dad, and he clears his throat.

"I've done things in my lifetime that I'm not proud of," Dad looks at me. "I'm still not the man I should be, but I'm trying. Which brings me to why I called you to dinner tonight and why Charity is here." Dad looks at Shana, and she nods for him to continue. "It may not have seemed so, but my children are my pride. I may have held on too tight, but I've always tried to do what was right. Brian's birth was life-changing. It made me reevaluate what and who I hold dear. Tonight, I right a wrong that stemmed long ago. Victoria, Devlin," Dad pauses. "Charity is your sister."

Eve coughs into her hands, then takes a sip of water from the glass in front of her. "Excuse me," She apologizes.

I imagine our thoughts are similar.

*What the hell?*

My confession pales in comparison to Dad's.

"Charity's mother and I were together for a year before she broke it off," Dad continues. "I won't go into detail. It was no one's fault. We just wanted different things, but Charity is a product of love. It was before I met Shana, of course." Dad hints at a smile when he glances at Shana, an action I haven't seen between them before.

I never even knew of Dad and another woman until Shana. It's his best-kept secret. I wonder what he promised Charity to keep quiet.

"My sister," Vicky says, unbelieving.

"Tonight has been full of surprises," Dad says, glancing at me. "It's a lot to take in for all of us. For now, let's eat and work through the heavy stuff in time." He lifts a brow, and I nod.

I'm willing if he is.

# Chapter 29

**Evelyn**

DEVLIN AND HIS family should get an award. No. More than one.

That was the most awkwardly surprising, frustrating, and confusing dinner I've ever attended. I've decided that from here on out, secrecy is not the way to go.

I stare out the window into the dark sky as Devlin drives me home.

I haven't spoken to him since we left his father's home, and he's allowed my silence, as he should. The words threatening to leave my mouth are not pretty and not nice. Devlin's secret was not a little thing to be taken lightly, and he kept it from me like it was of no concern. I was bombarded, and I'm pissed, but not only at him. There had to have been a sign somewhere for me to recognize. I feel like I should've known.

And Charity. I release a low grin at the thought. She's the second sister I mistook for a floozy. My head needs some serious examination after tonight.

"Eve," Devlin says when he turns onto my driveway. "Can we talk?" He asks.

"Can we not?" I counter, pushing the car door open when he stops. I step outside, righting my purse on my shoulder.

"We need to talk about this, Eve," Devlin says.

"I know, but not tonight," I said. I close the car door and walk away.

I meant what I said. I love Devlin more than I thought I could, but I don't like him very much right now.

I go inside and close the door behind me without looking back. While I get comfortable, slipping on shorts and a shirt, I call Holland. Within thirty minutes, he pulls into my driveway. He's always there when I need him.

"What is it this time?" Holland asks, stepping across the threshold into my house. He's crunching on M&Ms again.

"Those things are gonna rot your teeth," I told him.

"Maybe," Holland shrugs. "Now, where's the fire?"

"It's Devlin."

Holland swallows the pieces in his mouth. "Did he hurt you? Do I need to kick his ass because I will?"

"Yes. No. All of the above." I plop down on the couch, tilting my head to the ceiling.

"What happened?" Holland sits next to me.

"He's not perfect," I said.

"No one is perfect," He grins.

"He's more complicated than I thought." I continue blinking at the ceiling.

"As you should have expected," Holland says. "You've known Devlin for years, but you don't know *him*. True transparency doesn't happen overnight. It comes in time. It comes in spurts, sometimes in waves too high to handle in a single moment."

"I know. I just didn't expect Devlin to throw a grenade in the window as I tried to see my way through. I mean… His father is my boss," I said incredulously. "And the woman I thought stole the party out from under me every year actually didn't. Apparently, Mr. Sawyer gave it freely. I never stood a chance with the boss's daughter in the running." I sat up straight, huffing out a breath.

"Hmm?" Holland murmurs.

I look at him. "As I said. Way more complicated than anticipated."

"That's…." Holland pauses. "Did he say why he didn't tell you?"

"I didn't give him a chance, but does it really matter? He left out something important that concerned me. How do I know he won't do it again?" Anger and disappointment stir inside me.

"He probably will," Holland says with little doubt. "But don't you think he deserves the chance to explain?"

"You're not helping, Holly."

"Guess I deserved that," Holland Smiles. "Look, all I'm saying is, maybe he had a good reason past your understanding. You should hear him out. If not for him, for you. You deserve the full picture." He taps my knee. Then, he leans back and pops an M&M into his mouth.

I give Holland the side eye. "You're supposed to be on my side," I told him.

"I'm always on your side, and I'll always be here for you, but you need to talk to Devlin," Holland says. "Your relationship with him feels different than the last. This one actually cares, and he wants *you* to be known. Guys don't take *mean times* home to meet their parents. You're the lucky one."

"You call this luck?" I ask.

"I'd say you're more fortunate than most. And a little advice…."

"On top of the wonderful advice you've already given me," I snip jokingly.

Holland smiles. "I love meeting like this, but if your relationship is going to survive, you can't rely on me at the first sign of danger. Devlin may say he's not jealous, but he's a man. I'm a man. I know how I'd feel if I were in his shoes. Try working through things with him first. I'd hate for you to let him go because of me," Holland boasts.

"And who says you won't be the one I let go of?"

Holland's brows rise to his hairline.

"Yeah, you're probably right," I grin.

I ARRIVED AT WORK fifteen minutes late this morning to be sure I didn't run into Devlin. He had a meeting at eight that he couldn't miss now that he is in charge. I'm not ready to face him.

Recent events still haunted my dreams last night, waking me in a cold sweat, and Mr. Sawyer was at the forefront. He made no decisions at dinner, but his eyes spoke volumes. He wasn't happy, for sure. So, my life still hangs in the balance. What will he do now that he knows about Devlin and me?

I've gone over many scenarios and keep coming back to one. I should be the one to break it off with Devlin before anyone else finds out. It's what's best for both of us. I can't keep us in a position where he has to decide between my future and his own.

I look up from my computer screen when I sense a dark presence around me. My eyes widen, and my back straightens. I rise from my chair, brushing my hands over my dress.

"Mr. Sawyer. You're here," I said. I stare, picking his features apart for any resemblance to Devlin, but find none.

"Please, Evelyn. Sit," Mr. Sawyer says, raising his palm to me.

"If you're looking for Devlin, he's in a meeting." I sat as he instructed me, keeping my attention on him.

"I know. That's why I came. I wanted to speak with you alone." Mr. Sawyer walks further inside. "Mind if I sit?"

"Not at all, Sir. It's your property," I said with more sass than intended.

Mr. Sawyer hints a smile, then sobers. He sits in front of me, crossing his fingers over his lap. "It's quite the predicament we're in, Evelyn. Situations like yours and Devlin's need to be handled delicately. Otherwise, it may cause a company-wide rift, and I can't have that."

"I know, Sir. I never meant to jeopardize you or your company. I know the rules. I was wrong, and I'm prepared to take whatever punishment you deem fit."

"I'm glad you feel that way. It shows courage, a redeeming quality," Mr. Sawyer says. "I find myself in a personal predicament as well, Evelyn. This company was my dream, not Devlin's, and he would give it all up for you in a heartbeat. He may not believe it, but I love him too much to let that happen."

"So, where do we go from here?" I asked.

"I chose to let Devlin run the business, and that's what I'll do. As far as I'm concerned, he decides what happens next. I won't intervene. I'm his father first. Regardless of his decision, I trust you'll do what's right for you. You're a smart woman, Evelyn. He's lucky to have you," He pauses for a moment. "I was taught not to make decisions out of love, but I suppose that won't work for you in this instance. Love should be your deciding factor."

I stared, speechless and confused. I hadn't expected Mr. Sawyer's visit, let alone his response. He wants me to decide if Devlin's and my love is strong enough to withstand time. That's hard to gauge at any point in a relationship.

"Thank you, Mr. Sawyer," I said finally. "You've given me a lot to consider."

"I've taken enough of your time," Mr. Sawyer says, standing. He walks toward the door, stops, and turns back once he's there. "For what it's worth, Evelyn, if you were to choose love, I couldn't think of anyone more fitting for my son."

My mouth parts as Mr. Sawyer leaves. He's not as scary as I thought.

# Chapter 30

**Devlin**

THERE'S A MAJOR downfall to being in charge. I can't skip out on meetings that I initiate.

The Execs settle into the chairs around the table in the conference room along with Charity.

After a long talk with Sawyer about Robert and further investigation, he decided to replace Robert with someone he trusts.

"I'll keep this short," I said, addressing the room after they quieted down.

Most Execs know my relation to Sawyer, but Charity remains a secret until she's ready to reveal herself. I can't believe she's been in front of me this entire time, and I didn't know she was my sister. We need to discuss it at some point, but not now.

"If you haven't been notified, the Mintville location will be under new management effective immediately due to Robert's resignation," I continued.

Robert was accused of misconduct. He was allowed to privately resign and settle with his accusers or be terminated and have his name dragged through the mud. He chose the easy way out, and our employees were grateful they could remain anonymous from the public eye. As for the money he pocketed, he was ordered to return the money or face jail time. The shorted employees will receive an increase plus retro pay after careful review.

"Charity," I said, motioning to her, "will fill that position. Jan will step into Charity's role here." I smile at her. "I'll let you say a few words," I told her.

"Thanks, Devlin," Charity says.

Charity speaks, and everyone listens. I try, but she doesn't hold my attention. I can't stop thinking about Eve. She hasn't answered my calls and wasn't on time for work this morning. I'm worried about her and what she might do. I can't lose her.

All eyes focus on me when Charity is done.

"Is there anything further?" I address the room, my eyes meeting a few others. Everyone remains quiet. "Meeting adjourned," I said.

I'm the first one out of the conference room, warding off any late requests for my attention, but I'm not fast enough. "Devlin." Charity catches up to me, keeping pace with my steps. "I'd like to talk before I leave," she tells me.

I stop walking and look at her, and she stops with me. I glance at my watch as if I have somewhere I need to be.

"Yeah, sure. Let's do lunch in half an hour at Breck's," I suggested.

"Okay," Charity agrees, and we part ways.

I walk to Eve's office and stop outside her door, hoping she's here. Seconds pass before I round the door frame and stop just past the door. My heart beats easier at the sight of her sitting at her desk. I watch her closely, hesitant to speak and risk pushing her away.

Eve is focused on the papers on her desk, her eyes moving back and forth as if she's reading. "I can feel you watching me, Devlin," she says. I felt you the second you stopped outside my door."

Everything I want to say to her melts away when she looks at me. I see that I've hurt her, and I want to go to her and take it away somehow. I wish I could go back to the beginning and tell her everything before details got stacked and we became us—if there's still an us.

"I never meant to hurt you, Eve. I'm sorry."

"You should be," She scowls.

I glance over my shoulder. There shouldn't be anyone around, but I close the door from prying ears just in case.

"Nothing has changed, Eve."

"Yet, everything has," She responds. "You omitted the truth, Devlin. Tell me, what's your idea of a relationship? Because what you did was not ideal," She huffs.

I step closer to her desk, stopping an inch away as she continues.

"You asked me to trust you. How can I do that when you don't talk to me?"

"I wanted to protect you."

"You can't protect me from the truth," she says, her palm smacking the desk. "Your protection could have cost me everything." She stands, gives me her back, and walks to the window. Her arms fold around her middle.

I move behind Eve, enveloping her in my arms, and she squirms to be free.

"Let go of me, Devlin. I can't do this," Eve says with a faint crack in her voice.

"Is that really what you want?" I asked.

"It's, it's what I need," She sighs.

I kiss the back of her head, then release her, putting space between us. We stand in silence for a minute. When she doesn't turn around, I walk away, stopping when I reach the door. I hold the doorframe, looking at Eve's back.

"Don't write us off, Eve," I said before leaving.

CHARITY AND I MEET at Breck's and walk in together. The waitress from before gave me an unapproving glare as we neared the counter.

"Is there a story there?" Charity asks, glancing over her shoulder.

I grunt humorously. "She thinks I'm a jerk."

Charity grins. "Well, people think I'm a tease if it makes you feel any better. I guess bad aura runs in the family," She jokes.

We order a drink and sit.

"So, you're my sister," I said, breaking the ice.

"I'm your sister," Charity confirms.

"How long have you known?"

"About a year before my employment."

"Why the big secret? Why didn't Dad tell me?"

"I asked him not to mention it."

My brows furrowed, and Charity continued.

"Our father was not my favorite person growing up, through no fault of his own. My mother lied to me and kept me from him. When the truth was revealed, and we finally met, he wanted to know me. Our relationship grew from there, and he offered me a job once I graduated college. I accepted but didn't want people to think I didn't deserve it. Shana knew, of course, but she respected my wishes."

I think back over the years I've known Charity. She's one of the few women I work with that neither openly flirted with me nor hated my guts. She's always been friendly and uninterested.

"It's strange," I said. "I just learned of you, and you're leaving. I understand your privacy, but I wish I had known sooner.

"I'm only a plane ride away. This isn't the last you'll see of me." She smiles.

"I'm holding you to that."

"I'd expect nothing less," Charity says. "We should probably get back to work."

"Yeah," I said, glancing at my watch.

We finish our drinks and exit the shop.

"See you at the office," I told Charity.

"See you there," She replies. "And, Devlin. Tell Evelyn to keep the party going." She smiles and walks away.

I LEFT EVE ALONE for the remainder of the day as she wished. Now that I know we're alone in the office, I want to

288

go to her, but I don't. I stay in my office, waiting for her to leave, to avoid confrontation.

I lean my chair back and kick my feet up on the desk. I stay in that position until Eve's name lights the screen on my work phone. I let it ring two times before I answer to appear nonchalant.

"Devlin speaking," I answered.

Eve breathes into the line, then says, "I need to see you in my office." She ends the call before I can respond.

Being summoned is usually a sign of a problem. On my way to Eve's office, I hope that's not the nature of her request. I enter and close the door, expecting the best, unprepared for the worst.

Eve sits behind her desk, and when our eyes meet, an unsteady breath leaves me.

"You wanted to see me," I said, stopping at the corner of her desk.

"Thank you," Eve says.

I cock my head slightly, thrown off by her words. "For?"

"Everything. For giving me time to think. For my time here at MS Toys. For making room for me to fall in love with you," Eve says, looking down at the white envelope in front of her. She traces her fingertips over it, then stands, picks it up, and holds it toward me. "I can't be a secret any longer, and I won't stay and put your company at risk," she says.

I stare at the envelope, then at Eve. I walk around the desk and take the envelope from her, ripping it in half.

"I don't accept," I said, throwing the envelope in the trash.

"What do you mean you don't accept?" Eve blanches.

"I'm not letting you go, Eve.

"You have to."

"I can't."

"But your father said…."

"Fuck what my father said. We write our own rules, remember?" I hold the side of her arms, and she stares at me, her eyes searching mine.

"Your father said I should let love choose."

When did she speak with my father? I swallow that bit of information to decipher later.

"And do you love me still?" I rub my palms over her arms.

"I do." Eve turns away from me. "But I can't let you risk everything for me."

I step around her, so we're face to face again. "The biggest risk of all is letting you walk away. We've both fallen, Eve. I'm head over heels in love with you. Now, I'm asking you to stay. Stay in love with me."

Eve's eyes cloud over. "Devlin," She whispers.

"If you want me to get on my knees and beg, I will," I said, dropping to one knee. "Just, please, say you'll stay." I take her hand in mine, pressing my lips to her skin. "We don't have to remain a secret," I told her. "Marry me, Eve, because my life wouldn't be the same without you."

Eve sucks in a breath and drops to her knees in front of me. Her hands surround my face as our eyes kiss. Then, her lips press softly against mine as she nods and whispers, "Yes."

# Epilogue

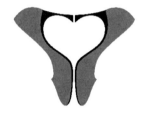

*One Year Later*

**Evelyn**

I HUFF OUT a long breath, typing memories of us into my digital diary. I smile at my handy work when familiar hands squeeze my shoulders. I tilt my head back.

"Hey. I was just thinking about you," I said to the handsome man behind me.

"Is that so?" Devlin steps around the recliner and kneels in front of me. "What are you working on?"

"Our story," I said, setting my laptop on the table next to me. "I just finished the part on how you ruined Christmas."

Years later, the events of that day are still fresh on my

293

mind. That was the night everything started to change. It's been a whirlwind ever since. Keeping a record of how we began seemed like a good idea. I never want to forget how Devlin and I got here. And if we ever have children, they'll get a kick out of our history, sans the intimate details.

Devlin parts my thighs and inches forward. "In my defense, you were the one who pushed me."

"True, but we never would've been in the closet if it weren't for you."

Devlin takes my hand in his, bringing it to his lips. "I'd say everything worked out for the better. Don't you think?" He pulls my ring finger into his mouth and sucks.

Our wedding is another day I'll never forget. Devlin and I got married at his father's home six months ago. It was an intimate gathering with only family surrounding us. My father gave me away while my mother looked on. My sister, Holland, and Devlin's family were all there. Even Charity made the trip.

Devlin and I planned our wedding in secret, and remained discrete on the job until we were married. Shock is the word I'd use to described our coworkers once we made the announcement. When Susan looks at me now, it as if she's asking me why, and I respond with a smile, keeping the answers to myself. She wouldn't understand, even if I tried to explain it.

"Well, yeah, but that doesn't change the facts," I

answered.

"Hmm. Facts," Devlin repeats. "I've wanted you from the moment I saw you, Eve. I'll always want you, even after we're old and gray. The party didn't go as planned, but it brought us closer together." He stands and pulls me up with him, resting his hands on my hips. "Be sure to add how I saved the night, will you?"

"I think it's perfect the way it is," I teased.

Devlin smirks, lifting my chin and running his thumb across my lips. "What do you say we reenact the final chapters?"

"I'm all for it on one condition. We start with the kiss in the closet." I wiggle my brows.

Devlin wraps his arms around me, pulling me closer. "You don't have to tell me twice, Mrs. Hughes."

"I like the sound of that. It makes me all warm and fuzzy," I told him.

"Do you now? Mrs. Hughes. Mrs. Hughes. Mrs. Hughes," Devlin repeats.

My body began to tingle as his lips descended upon mine. I close my eyes and fall into his kiss. He makes me feel every part of him, just as he'd done in the closet, and I push him away, reenacting the scene. Only this time, he won't let me go. He holds on, pulls me back, and kisses me again.

We're both gasping for air when we pull apart.

"You wear your name very well, Devil," I said, reciting a line from our story.

"And you know how to play your part, Eve."

Devlin captures my lips again, and I fall deeper.

It's hard to imagine a life where I'm not in love with Devlin. He challenges me in a way I've never been before. He keeps me distracted, and I don't mind giving him control when it's necessary. Our beginning was tense, but it was worth it. We had years of foreplay to get us to this point, and every moment of that time spent with him was unforgettable. That time made us inevitable.

Together Devlin and I learned what it means to love and be loved. And because of him, I know what it's like to wake up every morning and feel my home lying next to me.

# Acknowledgments

To my family,
Thank you for your making my life easier just by being you.

To Mary, Ebony, Parker's Angels,
Thank you for continuing to support me. My voice is heard because of you.

To Itsy Bitsy Book Bits,
Thank you for your invaluable service. It's always a pleasure working with you.

To all of the bloggers, authors, and everyone who had anything to do with this book's release, I thank you from the bottom of my heart. My words exist in the hands and hearts of many because of your hard work in helping to promote.

# Author's Note

Everything that anyone does, big or small, plays a huge part in an author's success. I appreciate you all so very much. Thanks for coming along with me on my journey. If you enjoyed reading my book, please consider posting a review on your preferred site; and don't forget to tell your friends about me.

# Until Next Time...

# About The Author

Angela K. Parker is an author who believes in HEAs. She writes intense romance with heart, emotion, and steam brought to life by strong heroines and their swoon-worthy heroes.

Angela lives in South Carolina. Amongst writing, she has a passion for reading, music, and math. When she's not engaged in any of the above, she's spending time with her family or catching up on the latest movies. She's always had an active imagination. Now she's putting it to good use.

# Connect With the Author

Visit <u>www.angelakparker.com</u> and sign up for Angela's newsletter to be informed of future releases.

Email: angelaparkerauthor@gmail.com